CW00503867

LADIES WH

When Women Get Together

mischief

This novel is entirely a work of fiction.
The names, characters and incidents portrayed in it are
the work of the author's imagination. Any resemblance to
actual persons, living or dead, events or localities is
entirely coincidental.

Mischief
An imprint of HarperCollins*Publishers*
77–85 Fulham Palace Road,
Hammersmith, London W6 8JB

www.mischiefbooks.com

A Paperback Original 2013

First published in Great Britain in ebook format by
HarperCollins*Publishers* 2012

Copyright
Ginger © Rachel Randall
Heartless © Alegra Verde
Bride to Be © Izzy French
Bump and Spike © Cammy May Hunnicutt
The Beach House © Liz Coldwell
Morning Glory © Giselle Renarde
Under the Slippers © Annabeth Leong
The Fruits of the Forest © Rose de Fer
The Hungry Eye © Emelia Rawlings
School for Popular Girls © Heather Towne

The author asserts the moral right to
be identified as the author of this work

A catalogue record for this book is
available from the British Library

ISBN-13: 9780007553419

Set in Sabon by FMG using Atomik ePublisher from Easypress

Find out more about HarperCollins and the environment at
www.harpercollins.co.uk/green

All rights reserved. No part of this publication may be
reproduced, stored in a retrieval system, or transmitted,
in any form or by any means, electronic, mechanical,
photocopying, recording or otherwise, without the prior
permission of the publishers.

Contents

Ginger
Rachel Randall

The old-fashioned bell on the door sounds as Lila lets herself in, its tinkle overlaying the distant drone of hairdryers and the gusting October wind from the street she's gladly left behind her. Warmth rushes to meet her, welcoming her in as she loosens her scarf with relief.

There's no one behind the reception desk, no sign of *her*, but as Lila shrugs off her coat onto the wrought-iron rack a woman calls, 'Be right with you. Make yourself at home.' Her voice is husky – hospitable, like the squashy sofa in the bow window, and unexpectedly dramatic, like the bowl of gaudily wrapped chocolates on the table with the magazines.

Lila breathes in the chemical tang of the lotions and potions, along with the fading perfumes of previous clients. She absorbs the pleasurable familiarity of a well-kept hair salon, revelling in the anything-is-possible moments before she's seated in the chair. And she reaches for the chocolates, because, after all, she's here to be indulgent.

Heels click on the varnished wood floor. Lila glances up from the frivolous trinity of *Heat, Hello* and *Time Out* to find that the woman who dared her to come is as striking as she remembers. Jeanne wears a scoop-necked black dress with three-quarter-length sleeves and a hem that flirts with her dimpled knees. Her shoes are mint-green Mary Janes with a round wooden mid-heel, and she's tied a matching scarf around her neck in a saucy side bow. The green is the right shade to turn her pale skin to peachy. And there's lots of skin; so much of it, at that neckline, that it's nearly, *nearly*enough to distract from the glorious cascade of her wavy red hair. The colours, her lushness, her magnetism, are such a contrast to the sterile hospital corridors where Lila's spent most of this day that she has difficulty tearing her gaze away.

Just like when they first met, last week at a pub in Marylebone. Lila was there with some colleagues from University College Hospital. There'd been a chorus of greetings to an acquaintance of an acquaintance – Jeanne – who'd shifted her own G&T to their table.

Lila noticed her hair first. It was lit by fire from the autumn sun, and her hands itched to touch it. When Jeanne noticed that Lila's hair was red too, though a more coppery shade, her polite smile turned mischievous.

'I know exactly what I want to do with you,' she said. 'Come see me next week, same day and time.'

Lila's pulse sped at the note of collusion in her voice. She automatically took the offered card and noticed gold-embossed shears in a top corner.

'What did you have in mind?' she asked. Their knees brushed under the table as people shifted seats around them. She let the contact linger.

'A private consultation.'

Jeanne's mouth curved in unmistakable invitation and Lila knew then that she would go, if only to feel the intensity of Jeanne's attention on her skin like that again.

In the here and now, Lila's anticipation flares into something fiercer and more immediate. *I remember you*, Jeanne's look is promising. *I have plans for you.*

'Hello,' Jeanne welcomes her, the syllables as warm and bright as the salon itself. 'You came.'

Not yet, Lila thinks, amused at her own lewdness, at her confidence about what's going to happen here. She's on edge, but pleasantly so. She's sparring, enjoying herself; it's been too long since she's felt this instant connection.

'Actually, I nearly didn't make it,' she jokes. 'Not with the Conran Shop so near. There's nothing I can afford there, but I always do like a good tease.'

Jeanne's smile reveals the little gap between her front teeth that Lila had been thinking about for seven days. 'I know,' Jeanne replies, '*exactly* what you mean.'

Lila finds herself moving forward without conscious memory of standing up. Jeanne takes her hand, her shiny plum fingernails dragging slightly over Lila's wrist before she releases her grip. Her face is faintly lined with laughter and about five years' more Octobers than Lila. She's beautiful – all beaming animation and expensive skin creams.

'I see you've discovered *my* weakness.' She arches a shapely brow at the pile of coloured foil discarded on the table before her blue eyes skim, blatant and interested, across Lila's cream blouse and navy trousers. 'My *other* temptation, I mean.'

Reaching into the bowl of chocolates, Jeanne drops a few into the pocket of her low-slung leather utility belt, next to all her scissors and combs. She peels back the wrapper on one and pops the chocolate into her red mouth. Lila watches Jeanne lick her lips, chasing sweetness, and she has the vivid sense memory of the rich texture of the chocolate fondant on her own tongue.

As she catches Lila staring, Jeanne walks to the door and turns both the latch and the sign to CLOSED. She jangles the tools in her belt, still smiling. 'Ready?'

The exposed brick walls of the salon are lined with tall, modern mirrors framed in gold. Lila watches their cascading reflections within them as Jeanne helps her on with a black cloak.

Once comfortably settled on the stylish leather chair, Lila keeps her eyes fixed on Jeanne's neck scarf. She traces the subtle pattern of the fabric up and down in its looping figure eight until these curves lead her to track the others on her stylist's body. The lush spread of her breasts, for instance, held firmly in place from the front but spreading decadently under the dress at the side-view, as though her lingerie can't quite contain them. Then on to rounded hips, shaped by the girdle of the leather belt and swaying as Jeanne moves in preparation behind her.

Jeanne murmurs, 'Your hair is beautiful.'

Lila's rush of pleasure at the compliment is intensified by the sudden sensation of fingertips grazing her temples. She nearly moans in approval at the lingering touch before Jeanne cards her hands through Lila's straight hair, pulling long strands through splayed fingers. The rolling motion of it is lazy, haphazard – almost like Jeanne's distracted by the colour, the texture – before settling into tugs too deliberate, too evenly timed, to be anything but by design.

Her eyelids feel heavy from the delights of this petting. They drift shut of their own accord, but she fights to open them, wanting to see Jeanne's expression as she assesses Lila's assets. Jeanne's reflection is studying her, her full lips parted just enough to show a hint of pink tongue. In the mirror she can see flashes of Jeanne's nails and the way Lila's own hair seems brighter in contrast as it skims over the polish. When Jeanne steps away, assessment over, Lila feels the sudden lack of contact acutely.

'Join me in the back?'

There's laughing invitation from Jeanne, just like there was at the pub. Lila feels like she's pressed up against the glass of that Conran Shop, looking in at all the expensive pretty things out of reach. Yet here she can walk right in and take what she wants. It's an intoxicating feeling.

In the back of the salon there's a spiral staircase leading up to a mezzanine, and a row of chairs slouching low before curving sinks. To Lila's over-sensitized skin, reclining into one feels like an embrace.

'How much will we be doing today?' Jeanne asks formally, her hands resting on Lila's shoulders.

It's a question about cut; it's a question about whatever Lila wants it to be.

'I think,' Lila says, 'I'll leave myself in your capable hands. I've heard that you would know exactly what to do with me.'

A low laugh that's part triumph, part promise. 'In that case, we have a new conditioner that I think you'll love,' Jeanne teases. 'Mint and rosemary. The scent's divine.'

God, her *voice*. She makes it sound like she's never seen anything so fascinating as Lila's hair. It makes Lila want to know what Jeanne will think of the rest of her, whether she'll get that husky note when considering Lila's breasts, or her bum. Will her touch there be this expert, too?

Mental note, Lila thinks, as Jeanne lifts the gauzy curtain veiling the back of the room and disappears to find the supplies: Do not let this gorgeous woman talk you into hundreds of pounds' worth of product. Though she can't fool herself. If Jeanne gives her that smile again, even at half the wattage, she'll be styling putty in this woman's hands and her nurse's salary be damned.

'Lie down for me.'

Lila responds instantly to the note of command in Jeanne's voice, her thoughts trailing off into one long arch of her back and tip of her head. Jeanne rubs a thumb down her throat in a long, rewarding caress before she begins to shampoo her without further comment.

Jeanne's hair falls in a warm curtain, smelling sweetly of woody spices and the alcohol tang of hairspray. Lila inhales deeply as Jeanne bends over her task.

'You like being touched.'

It's all too easy to simply moan in agreement. The water splashing the back of Lila's neck feels cooler against her suddenly flushed skin.

'Occasionally my clients fall asleep when I wash their hair,' Jeanne murmurs.

Lila's unsurprised, what with the stroking of strong fingers, the pounding of the water, and the soporific heat. But it's nearly impossible to imagine that she could sleep in this situation – on the contrary, every part of her is singing from proximity, from being the focus of this woman's careful attentions.

'Tell me if it's too hot.'

7

All of it's hot, but Lila has no plans to complain. Jeanne's hands keep up their excellent work. Her knuckles scrub vigorously across Lila's scalp, rubbing all thought from her mind. Everything goes deliciously blurry again and resistance is impossible against the onslaught of endorphins. She coasts on it, listening to the water and Jeanne's soft murmurs of approval, until she's dimly aware that her hair is being gathered into a towel. She's tingling, from root to tip, feeling cool and hot all at once. Her hair feels nice, too.

Unsteadily, she follows Jeanne up to the mezzanine over the main floor, clinging to the rail of the spiral staircase. In contrast, Jeanne moves confidently as she fetches Lila a glass of water and settles her into another leather chair.

Lila has never paid much attention to her hair. She wears it long from habit, keeping it out of the way on shift with a ponytail. It's always been easy to manage, being poker-straight and thick. And, most importantly, in the right light it's got enough gold in it for her to have avoided the worst of the schoolyard catcalls. Beyond summertime highlights and a few experimental fringes, she's never been particularly adventurous.

All that is swiftly changing, however. Jeanne pins up thick shanks of hair, choosing her starting point and tickling the lobe of Lila's ear with the edge of the comb as she brushes out more strands. There's something riveting

8

about the dangerous possibilities offered by the glinting scissors she reaches for next.

'Trust me,' Jeanne urges, and the blades flash.

Lila feels the tension-release of the metal through her hair an instant before the strands fall away. She stares dumbly at them, at the way they've fallen in disarray along the heavy cloth of the cape. Then she catches sight of herself in the mirror.

'Short,' she manages.

Jeanne's naughty grin is unrepentant. 'Take it like a good girl,' she counters, and snips again. And again, until the sudden nerves in Lila's tummy flutter in time to the staccato clicks. She can feel the cool metal against the back of her neck, blending with the brush of Jeanne's working hands. It's too early to see where this is going other than *ohmygod* short, yet she already feels exposed.

'When was the last time you had a proper cut?' Jeanne's razor-sharp scissors *snip*. Lila's locks yield, slanting to the floor as the bold cut takes shape.

'Too long,' she breathes, adrenaline transforming nerves into something dirtier.

Jeanne's breasts brush the side of Lila's skull as she sways close. 'Then I hope you're enjoying yourself.'

God, yes.

It's exhilarating, being a captive audience to her own seduction. The massive mirrors in front of her, around them, reveal everything in glorious, overwhelming detail.

9

Lila grows drunk on it – the sexy woman, the stylish room, the titillation of watching herself. Lila's lips are reddened. Parted. Her eyes widen, pupils dilating as she takes in every detail. And her hands …

At first she's content with gripping the edges of her chair, her nails digging into the leather every time Jeanne's careful touches nearly drive her to moan aloud. But her pussy is tingling – wet and very interested – and without conscious decision she's spreading her thighs underneath the protective black cape. She's hidden there, right in plain view, and the contradiction is thrilling. It's no effort at all to sneak her right hand down between her thighs to thumb open the buttons of her trousers.

Jeanne sets her scissors aside to pick up the hairdryer. Out of sight, Lila's fingers curl around the mound of her lace-covered pussy, feeling how she's already dampened her knickers. She toys with the elastic, teasing carefully. A rush of moisture sends her slouching lower in her seat, sighing.

There's a pause, and the heat dips away from her for a moment. Their eyes meet in the mirror, sky-blue on Lila's brown. Jeanne lets out a breathy little sound. When the dryer comes back, Lila bites her lip … and lets her fingers slide underneath her knickers. They glide, feather-light, across her bare clit.

'You enjoy it.' Jeanne strokes her index finger across one earlobe, drawing a shudder. Lila's own fingers skid, pressing to relieve the *wanting*. 'These rituals. Being tended.'

The lace is slick now. She wants to touch herself properly, skin on skin. She wants to think about Jeanne *tending* to her, but now Jeanne's flicking off the dryer and lowering it away. In the abrupt silence, she can hear the pounding of her heart in time to the insistent throbbing between her legs.

Jeanne cups her palm around her nape, squeezing gently. Lila gasps, tilting her head back immediately to deepen the touch. Jeanne indulges her with a few final strokes, then releases the lock on the chair and spins it around, so Lila's facing into the main room. After the intimacy of being trapped between Jeanne's warm body and her own reflection, the open space is jarring.

Jeanne holds up a small hand-mirror. When Lila doesn't move, still punch-drunk, she prompts, 'Give me your hand.' It's not a request.

Underneath the cape, Lila's right hand is slippery with her own arousal. With her left, she reaches for the mirror, trying to muster attention from her lust-crazed mind.

Her new haircut *is* short; cropped into a slanting little bob that flirts with her jaw and gives her cheekbones she's never noticed before. She looks sassy. She looks sexy. 'I love it,' Lila breathes. But even more, Lila loves that she's been colluding with this woman – a virtual stranger – to objectify her own body. She sets the mirror aside. 'Thank you.'

'Thank *you* for indulging me.' Jeanne leans very close,

like they might kiss. Instead, she flips aside the cape and stares down at Lila's lap, at the flush across her thighs and the white-knuckled pressure of her thumb still pressing beneath her knickers.

The cape drops to the floor. Jeanne folds herself after it, crouching down before her. Lila gasps when Jeanne's fingers finish opening her trousers. She's built straight up and down rather than with Jeanne's luscious curves, and it's the work of moments for Jeanne to ease the fabric down over her hips and away.

'You're –' there's a little crack in the word, a tremor from Jeanne that lets Lila know she's not alone in this '– even more stunning than I thought you'd be.'

Jeanne tilts fully into Lila's space, blue eyes intent and darkened by sex. She surges forward to take her mouth and the touch of lips on lips is messy, chaotic and *incredible*. Jeanne tastes like chocolate. Her lashes flutter and close, and they're cuts of amber over the shadowed cream skin beneath her eyes. There are faint freckles too. Lila notices them in the hazy moment before the sensations from the soft tongue stroking into her mouth smudge out all other thought.

The kiss goes on – wet and slippery, all-absorbing – until Lila becomes dimly aware that Jeanne is sliding her shears up, up, *up* her splayed thigh. She jerks away from the kiss as she feels the blunt outer edge of the blade furrowing her skin as it goes.

Jeanne asks, 'How much do you like your knickers?'

Lila is barely breathing from excitement. Across the room, the ornate mirrors reflect her desire back at her, amplifying it a thousand times. 'Do it. Please.'

The blades open, slicing through the lace; Jeanne moves with exquisite care to do the same to the other side.

Lila spreads her legs as wide as she can as Jeanne yanks the knickers free. Setting the shears aside, she rubs her fingertips across the path of the blades until Lila's sense-memory is overwhelmed by the new stimulation. There are little work calluses on her hands and they catch against Lila's smoother skin. Heavy waves of her red hair frame her face. She's unbearably *hot* and, for Lila, the rush of completely giving herself over to this woman is dizzying.

'Come here, that's it.' Jeanne urges Lila's legs up, encouraging her ankles to droop across her shoulders so that she's revealed to her liking.

Lila knows her own body well. She knows what she will look like to Jeanne, with her plump pussy dusted with coppery curls and her eager clit already flushed with blood and peeping from its hood. From this angle, she can see Jeanne absorbing all this new knowledge. Learning *her*. Lila was drawn to her competence from the start, loved the way it radiated from her and turned to blatant sexual energy between them. Now she's on fire with wanting more.

13

'I'm going to lick you. I want to taste you. Let me?' Jeanne's tongue darts out over her lips.

Lila whines, already anticipating the feel of it. 'Don't tease ...'

In simple answer, Jeanne opens her luscious mouth against her.

Lila's hips judder in shock but Jeanne holds her steady, curling her fingers into the flesh of her bum to keep her right where she's wanted. Her tongue curls, too, sliding across already slick flesh before fully exploring Lila's exposed folds. It's overstimulation of the best kind, amplifying her need into an inarticulate shout that echoes in the empty salon.

Jeanne draws back, her mouth glistening and amused. 'What if people come in and hear you?'

Lila lets her head fall back against the edge of the chair. Her eyes flutter shut as the edge of a fingernail tickles before her inner thigh is soothed by a damp kiss. 'I'll tell them I really recommend that shampoo.'

The answering laugh turns to more kisses. More and more, until they all blend into one intimate, open-mouthed kiss. This onslaught of tongue and lips and suction ceases only when Jeanne needs to breathe; even then, she rubs her cheeks against Lila's thighs, like she doesn't want to stop touching her even through her heavy panting.

Come and saliva slick her pussy and thighs. Now there

are delicate fingers pressing just inside her, making her desperate for more. Her clit feels stiff and huge. Jeanne is lavishing her attention on the nub, tickling it and teasing it with the tip of her tongue before sealing her mouth over it to suck. She backs off again only to repeat the entire process. It's amazing, all of it; Lila's finding it impossible to process, she's blindingly aroused. Her thighs quiver as her hands tangle in the soft fall of Jeanne's hair. She bucks, wanting more contact directly on, *in*, her pussy, but Jeanne doesn't give it to her. She just keeps sucking at her clit with rhythmic bursts of pressure that send Lila thrashing and wild.

Lila fists Jeanne's hair, yanking roughly. Jeanne ignores it. She *sucks*, and Lila surges over the cliff of her orgasm. Pleasure wracks her body. Jeanne's tongue strokes roughly across her trembling pussy, coaxing more aftershocks, until Lila cries out.

'Enough, enough –'

Jeanne pulls away and wipes her mouth with the back of her hand. Her expression is indulgent as she shifts off her knees and stands. 'Mmm. Just relax for me for a moment.'

Lila bonelessly obeys, her legs falling without Jeanne to hold her up.

It's only a matter of minutes, however, before Jeanne returns. If Lila's feverish brain is expecting anything, it's a towel and some clean-up. What she's definitely *not* expecting is the heavy slap of the back of a hairbrush across her bare thigh. Rather than rattling her out of her post-orgasmic haze, the thrilling shock of it rockets her into desire once more again.

The brush bristles look like they will scratch against thin tender skin. She thinks for a strung-out moment that Jeanne will do it. She tenses.

'Ease back, love. Not today.'

Lila stares at the hairclips that Jeanne has carelessly stowed on the low-cut collar of her dress. She looks at their clamping teeth then down at the erect nipples distorting her own blouse.

'Next time?'

A low chuckle as Jeanne hitches Lila's legs back up into position.

Lila's so wet that the handle of the hairbrush – smooth, thick, tapered – slides inside her immediately. She clamps around it instinctively, so tight that Jeanne murmurs as she tries to stroke it deeper.

'Shh. Let me fuck this into you.' There's a bead of perspiration on Jeanne's temple and hectic colour high on her cheeks. 'Give me the rest of your cream, because I know you have more for me.'

Jeanne's fingers flex against the brush and Lila's glassy stare is riveted to the movement. She imagines those capable fingers, stretching her. Curling inside her. Rubbing the spot, *this spot*, that the handle is grazing with blunt, clumsy strokes. She loosens, just enough for Jeanne to push further. Lila groans, head tossing back and forth.

'*Yes*,' she pleads.

'Stop ruining your new hair.' Jeanne's laughing command is choked, the sound of it bitten off. Her left hand works quickly, pushing and pulling on the brush with rough momentum. She licks the fingers of her right and rubs them with equal speed across the shiny swell of her clit.

It feels so good to have the thick length inside her … all Jeanne.

This time her orgasm is effortless; it flows over her, leaving her instantly limp.

'Oh, oh,' she hears Jeanne groaning in sympathy. 'Take more –'

She lets her body go, giving it all up to her. Her eyes open again to find Jeanne looking somewhere between satisfied and starving.

'You were right,' Lila says when she's breathing evenly again. She lowers her shaky feet to the ground and urges Jeanne up into her lap. She grins at the other woman, holding her tightly. 'You did know exactly what to do with me. How is that?'

'We gingers need to stick together.' Jeanne's hair is dishevelled, as devil-red as her swollen lips.

Lila explores her own hair. It feels good. Light and

immediately comfortable. 'So … how often will I need a cut and, ah, blow?'

'Often.' Jeanne's cat's eyes gleam. 'High-maintenance, that style.'

'Good,' Lila tells her, because it's *very* good. 'I was hoping you'd say that.'

Heartless
Alegra Verde

I met her at a party. She was … lovely, so perfect, like one of those cakes with butter crème icing so lush and pretty that you want to dip your finger in for a taste, but the tip of your finger hovers just above it because you don't want to mar its beauty. She had that look: confident, chin high, eyes cool, untouchable. Made me want to touch her all the more. Long smooth legs, I wanted to stroke them. I wondered if she was strictly straight, or if she might be more adventurous.

I liked the way she moved, the delicate bend of her wrist, the way she shrugged and tilted her head when she laughed. Although nearly model-thin, she was easily a C cup and her ass was peach-ripe; made drool gather in my mouth and my teeth clench. I'd watched as she made her way around the room once before finding a spot to rest. Her café con leche skin was just a shade deeper than the pale olive most Americans attribute to Latinas, and her hair was a mass of dark, loose curls that fell to the middle of her back.

The night was a purple sky, stars, and a sweep of skyscrapers that framed her as she leaned into the right side of the nearly floor-to-ceiling window casing. Her dress, a slip of raw rose-coloured silk, barely covered the necessities. When she occasionally shifted from one leg to the other, the slippery fabric dipped into the crevice the movement created between her legs. A neglected spaghetti strap slid down her arm as she raised a tall frosty glass to her lips.

She'd hardly paused before they'd begun paying homage. I stood on the other side of the room sipping a beer and watching her hold court. Men and women stopped before her, smiling and offering eager conversation, their eyes wide, faces animated. Her face remained unaffected: a nod, a word, a brief shake of her head. Rejection. They moved on. I imagined she saw me, looked at me from across the room. Her eyes assessing, probing, measuring my worth. I smiled. She didn't.

A man approached her. He wore a dark, very nice Hugo Boss, and a haircut that allowed a swatch to fall over his eye in just the right way. He leaned against the wall, towering over her. He spoke to her, but he didn't look at her. She didn't look at him. She said something that made him stop and look down at her, long. Then, smiling, he turned his back to her, but he didn't move away as his eyes scanned the crowd again. He spoke again as though addressing air before turning back to her. Extending a large slow hand, he touched the hem of her dress. Finally, the tips of his broad fingers touched her inner thigh and slid slowly up up up until his wrist was suspended just under the slip of rose silk, his hand completely hidden. She didn't move. I held my breath. I could feel my nipples straining against the fabric of my blouse. After what seemed minutes, but was probably only a few seconds, he pulled his hand away, brought his fingers to his nose and breathed in her scent. He leaned in and whispered something into her ear, his mouth pressed to the dark curls that fell around her neck. She shook her head, and he straightened, returned to his post on the wall near her. The fabric of his expensive suit fell flawlessly back into place as did the bored look on his aristocratic face, but he didn't move on.

The heat rose in my groin and, although I held myself still, I couldn't help squirming a bit as I leaned against the wall on my side of the room. The man in the Hugo Boss pulled his phone out of an inside pocket and called someone. He spoke quickly, still scanning the room. He turned to her again. She listened for a moment and nodded. He held his hand out to her and she took it. I watched as they crossed the room, he acting as navigator and she floating close behind as they waded through the crowd. I sipped my beer. As they drew nearer, I dropped my eyes, not wanting her to see me gawking. Her feet were smooth, a lean line that ended in a slanted plane of glistening crimson-blush-coloured toenails and strappy spiked heels. They were so near I could smell her perfume, something soft and clean like spring. I breathed her in. She stopped, the sway of the crowd pressing her closer.

'Come along.' Her voice was a breath of something distant like mangoes, citrus and a breeze off the Atlantic.

I looked up and she was there in front of me, all dark eyes and sweet breath aimed at me. My lower lip dropped before I could catch it. Another moment passed before I snapped my mouth shut. She nodded and took my hand. I followed.

* * *

The Hugo Boss guy, who I later found out was a stock-broker named Adam Cruz, took us back to his place, a good-sized apartment off Central Park. She was Lira Sands, a model. Up close, when I could see her eyes, I remembered her from a Max Factor eyeshadow campaign a couple of years ago. There had been a very memorable billboard in which she'd worn a veil over her mouth and all you could see was a pair of haunting hazel eyes. The eyes were just as spectacular up close.

Adam poured drinks, wine for Lira, another beer for

me, and what appeared to be Scotch neat for himself. Drinks in hand we followed him over to a huge, richly upholstered play pit. He sank onto one of the thickly cushioned units, sprawling with his back to the incredible view of the Park below as Lira slid in next to him. I sat across from the two where I could enjoy the view. Adam pointed a remote control at a series of panels on the wall and jazz, something interwoven with muted horns and an occasional Mingus bass, deep and throaty, began to play. After about twenty minutes, there was a knock at the door and he came back with what must have been a couple of ounces of coke. This was apparently why she'd come because the smile that she beamed up at Adam was large and genuine when he sat down next to her and began to prepare the lines.

He handed the sheet of clear plastic with its rows of white lines and the tightly rolled twenty-dollar bill to her and the lines disappeared. She pinched her nose, swiped at it a bit and smiled over at me. I smiled back, I think. Adam and I did a few lines while she took her little beaded bag to the bathroom. When she came back, she sat between Adam and me. She had already slid the straps of her dress off her shoulders; they hung just beneath her arms. She pushed the dress down, pressing it beneath her breasts so that the rose-coloured silk framed the succulent cream-coloured globes. A slight movement and they bounced free of their confinement. They were

23

buoyant and eager, the tips tight and brown. The neck of my beer bottle halted, poised on my lower lip waiting. She had my attention. Leaning forward, she trailed a finger down a line of white powder, rubbed the finger over her nipples, and turned towards me.

I put the bottle down and lowered my mouth to the jutting buds. They were hard and hot. She pulled me closer, running her fingers through my newly cropped hair. I sucked harder; she moaned and squirmed, pulling me down onto her as she fell further into the gold satin of the play pit. Adam was above me kissing her mouth. Now she had one hand in his hair too. I slid one of my hands along the length of her thigh, the flesh firm, soft and warm. She slid her legs open and my hand slipped over and along her inner thigh. My fingers moved up, caressing the smooth warm skin, the tight flesh, as she squirmed approvingly. Her inner thighs, just beneath her sex, were moist, a fact that made me extremely happy. The thin line of hair that trailed down the V of her sex did little to shield her damply swollen labia. I stroked the line, petting the sweet puss, and then trailed a long finger over her wet nether lips before sinking it into the depths of her hot, sticky wetness. She bucked, trying to press her sex further onto my stiff finger. I slid a second finger in. As she pressed, trying to pull them deeper, I sucked the other nipple, nipped it with my teeth, the coke causing my lips to tingle and feel slightly swollen.

Adam was still kissing her, but his hand had found its way down the back of my pants. He was gripping and squeezing the cheeks of my ass and sliding a couple of rough and gentle fingers down the crevice to tuck them under my ass and tease the sensitive skin between my legs. I was a little surprised, but it felt good so I let him.

'Take them off,' he said against my hair and then he stood up and began removing his jacket and then his shirt.

I sat up, a little dazed, and did as he asked. My pants made a dark puddle on the floor that pooled into Adam's. He stood over us, naked now, his engorged sex heavy and thick, the dark hood straining upward. I massaged the dampness that saturated my panties, stroking my labia and teasing my clit, before drawing them off and kicking them into the puddle.

Lira sat up and began on the buttons of my blouse. She leaned in and sucked at my lower lip, nipped at it and then slid her tongue in deep and slow. I sucked on her tongue whenever she slid it in, while my fingers, imitating her tongue, slid against her sex, slipping between the moist lips. I could feel her smile in the beginning, but as her thrusts became more insistent she made little mewling noises and tugged at my sleeves. Then she was on her back and Adam was pushing the skirt of her dress up around her hips, revealing the thin arrow of hair and swollen vulva that I had been teasing with my fingers. Her legs parted and the layers of plump pink lips fell

25

open. Adam sprinkled bits of white dust over them. He lowered his head to her breasts and left the sprinkled confection for me. I lapped it up and slid my tongue, long and slow, along the seam before finding her jutting little clit to lick and suck and tug. She squirmed and pressed her sex into my face. I held onto her hips and continued to nip and lick as she bucked.

Lira's hands were pulling at my hair and Adam was stroking my bare back, his fingers running along the knobs of my spine and finally moving down to cup my ass as I slid up the length of Lira's body, her chest to mine. Pushing my thigh between her legs, I pressed it hard against the sensitive tissue of her sex while I slid my sex against the firm flesh of her thigh. My breasts were tight, the nipples screaming hard as they tried to pierce her skin. She squirmed beneath me and I pressed my thigh deeper, pressed my breasts into hers. Her softness pooled around me. She grabbed at my ass, my back, her nails scraping, trying to gain a grip. I plunged my tongue into her mouth. She sucked it eagerly, pulling me into her. I pressed myself tighter, her wetness and mine coming and spilling as I rode her until she cried out and I saw trembling streaks of white.

I sank into her body, relishing the soft supple flesh, but after a minute or so she slipped out from under me.

'I'm going to do another line,' she said as she stood up. 'Adam wants to fuck you, OK.'

He was behind me stroking my ass again. How long had he been there? He pressed his condom-covered cock into the crevice of my ass, the knob against my anus.

'No,' I groaned and, scrambling up, I made an uncertain effort to move out from under him. I was nearly up on all fours as his hands gripped my hips.

'No?' he asked as if to confirm my choice. 'Maybe later.' And then he pressed the hood of his penis to the slick opening of my sex and pushed home, the whole of him rasping and pressing against the walls of my canal as he gripped my hips with his massive hands, his thumbs pressing into the flesh of my ass.

'So tight and hot,' he breathed. 'You haven't had a man in a while.' He pressed forward, his penis ramming its head against the depths of my womb. The feeling of fullness and the rhythmic slide of his flesh ignited a flash of need in my already trembling sex. Maybe it was the coke or maybe it was that my pussy was still pulsing from my last orgasm, but it felt good. I pushed back against him, wanting to feel the rasp and press of him as the hard heat stroked my walls. He pulled back and pressed himself into me slow and long, letting me feel the stroke and rub of him as he set a faster pace that had me writhing and pressing my pussy into his groin. I wanted to feel more of him. I wanted to feel the slap and heat of his sack, the agonising pleasure of the scratch and scrape of his groin hair against my hungry labia. His hands were

27

everywhere, stroking the length of my back, the crevice of my ass, pulling at the flesh and extremely sensitive skin of my hips and ass. He groaned, the sound punctuating the wet slapping rhythm. A vibration washed over me and a shudder rushed down the length of my body. He almost lost his grip, but he reclaimed a fleshy stronghold and the pace increased. His penis swelled and tightened, filling every inch of me with firm hot flesh. He slid a sly finger beneath me to press and stroke my swollen clit.

It was too much, the way he filled me, the rasp and pull of his cock along the walls of my sex, the slap of his sack against my tingling vulva, and the wide finger that pressed and pushed my screaming clitoris. My body tightened around his, my pussy squeezing him, sucking at him. He grunted and increased the pace, his hands gripping my hips, trying to steady my body for his assault. He was pounding into me and I was falling forward, my arms trembling, no longer capable of supporting me. I was a mass of tingling nerves. He grunted again, jerked and pulled me back, holding me to him, my rear to his groin. I could feel the rush as he came and came, his body stiff as his penis throbbed and surged forward. My sex vibrated around his, sending an electric wave through my body. I couldn't move, my arms and face and breasts splayed over a large segment of the play pit. And then he was falling forward, the lower half of my body collapsing beneath his.

I lay there, a mass of tingling nerves, insensate, for I don't know how long. After a while, Adam slapped my bottom lightly and said, 'I like fucking you.' With that, he got up and padded out of the room.

I nodded, but I couldn't talk just then.

* * *

Lira sat across from me, her legs curled under her. She was sipping a Diet Pepsi from a can. Her dress was in its proper place. The straps were even resting on her shoulders where they were meant to be. She had been watching us. There was a bit of white powder on the end of her nose.

'What's your name? I know you said, but I've forgotten.' She stretched her legs and feet out over the large square table that filled the open space in the middle of the pit.

'Ada,' I said sitting up and looking around trying to locate my clothes. They were wadded in the pile of clothing near the opening of the pit. We had apparently fucked our way to its centre. I tried scooting back down the cushions towards the clothing, but my bottom was wet and sticky and I didn't want to smear my juices all over the upholstery so I stood up, feeling quite self-conscious about my nudity when Lira sat across from me clothed.

Adam appeared wearing a dark-red cotton robe. He handed me its twin. I took it gratefully. It was smooth, brushed cotton, and large enough for me to tuck my feet under it when I sat down.

'Hungry?' he asked. I looked to Lira. 'Lira never eats. Chorizo and eggs?'

'I could eat,' I admitted.

'Juice or coffee?'

'Both.' He smiled, nodded, and headed into the kitchen.

A blue Miles was floating about the room, the sounds melancholy and strangely cleansing. Lira sipped her Pepsi.

'Why me?' I asked.

'I liked the way you looked at me,' she said without forethought.

'How?'

'Big eyes, dopey.' She sat her soda can on the table, pulled her knees up and leaned on them, her chin resting on her folded arms, her hands, beautiful and slender, peeking out. The nails were painted the same soft colour as her toes.

'Dopey?'

'Adoration. Lovestruck.'

I could feel the heat of embarrassment creeping up my neck.

'Don't be embarrassed. I'm used to it.'

'Are you and Adam ...?'

'Not really. We were once. It didn't work out.'

I felt myself nod at that, like some reporter amassing information.

'Do you often go with women?' I asked.

'Sometimes, but ... it's just that there is no ultimate reward, you know,' and she pressed her splayed fingers to the silky fabric that concealed her sex to emphasise her point, or lack thereof. 'But you were good. I enjoyed it with you.' Was she trying to appease me? 'Adam enjoyed you too. He came hard, and he's cooking for you.'

I didn't say anything. She watched me, quiet. I watched my feet and thought about the last hour.

'Do you often go with men?'

'No,' I said.

'You seemed to like it.' Her eyes bore into me.

'It was probably the coke.'

'Adam is good. He likes women.'

'And you? Do you like women?' I knew I was pressing her, but I had the evidence of her pleasure still glistening on my lips and thighs.

'Not particularly. I brought you for Adam.'

'I see.' What could I to say to that?

Adam was back with a tray heavy with two plates of eggs scrambled with spicy sausage, toast, orange juice and coffee. He pushed Lira's feet off the table and set the things out. It smelled good, hot buttered bread, pica spices and fresh-brewed coffee.

I dug in. He plopped down on the floor and followed suit. Lira sipped her Pepsi.

'So, Ada, what do you do?' Adam asked after swallowing.

'I sell books.'

'Books?' That from Lira. He cast her a shushing look.

'What kind of books?' Adam asked.

'I own a used bookstore.'

'How long have you owned it?'

'Nearly five years now. I bought it off a friend. She needed money for medical expenses. I was just going to run it for her, hold her place so to speak, and then she didn't need it any more.' The eggs were good. I wondered where he bought his chorizo.

'You don't like it?' I knew he meant the store and not the eggs. He had to see the way I was gobbling them down.

'Sometimes I love it, but the hours are long. Do you like being a broker?'

'Sometimes. It pays well. Do you have a woman, a lover?' Whatever happened to transitions? I chewed more slowly. Lira watched me. Adam took a large swallow of coffee and then another forkful of eggs, but I felt him waiting for my answer.

I swallowed. 'No.'

'No woman?' He ate some toast.

'No.'

'A man?'

'No.'

'How long?'

'How long what?'

'How long since you had a lover?'

'Why?'

'I like you. I like the way you feel.'

'This was fun, but it was a one-time-only event.'

'It doesn't have to be. You like Lira. You like me?' He sipped from his coffee cup, his eyes watching me over the brim.

'Lira doesn't like women.'

'Lira? Where did that come from?'

'She said so.'

'It's just that I have a lover, a husband actually,' Lira inserted.

'Then why are you here with us?' I didn't believe her or I didn't want to, and, even though I knew it was irrational, I was angry. 'If you're so content with this husband, why were you at Jack's party without him?' I didn't like that they had been working together to manipulate me. And worse, I didn't like that I had been so needy and that it had been so obvious.

'I told Adam I'd help him find someone. He doesn't like the bar scene. He's quite picky and he picked you. We picked you,' she said easily.

'Why me? Because you figured I'd be easy prey?'

'Because I like the way you wear your clothes, the loose fit of your trousers, the way they hang on your hips, the way your breasts push against the fabric of your blouse, the cut of your hair, the way it hugs your

33

head accentuating your cheekbones.' Adam watched me, his eyes on my face, as he spoke and then he took a sip from his coffee cup and was silent.

I wondered where he'd been when we were at Jack's, how he'd been able to watch like that, without me seeing him.

'I like that you fit just under my chin, that your body just slides into place. I could put my chin on top of your head without bending my knees – if you'd let me. Do you like anything about me?'

I didn't even have to think about it. 'The eggs are perfect,' I said, looking directly at him so that he could see the honesty in my face and the limits I was setting. He laughed anyway. Lira pursed her lips.

'Anything else?' His voice was strong, the same dusty baritone, and there was no whine, but the words felt like need. I thought about it, running through the last few hours, beginning with his hand under Lira's dress.

'Lira says you like women,' I offered.

'I do,' he confirmed.

'I believe you,' I said remembering how he'd stroked my clit to make sure I came before him and that he'd thought to bring me a robe afterwards. And that he hadn't pressed his advantage when he was behind me. Not fully, not this time anyway. I sipped my juice and watched him eat. Lira leaned over and tore off a piece of his toast.

'I liked the way you looked at Lira,' he continued as though there hadn't been a lull in the conversation. 'As though you wanted to swallow her whole. It made me jealous and I had to have you. Now that I have, I find that I want to keep you. At least, for a bit.'

'I'm not sure whether to be flattered or frightened.'

'Flattered, definitely,' he said, finishing his eggs.

Having eaten everything, I pushed my plate away, gathered my clothes into a manageable bundle and made my way to the guest bathroom I'd seen near the entryway. A few minutes later, I was fully clothed and ready to say my farewells. I figured I would shower when I got home. When I came out of the bathroom, Lira rose from her cushions to stand before me. She leaned down, pressed her lips to mine and slid the pointed end of her little tongue along the length of my lower lip.

'I like you. I really do, but this thing with Charlie is new. It's like I told Adam, I want to try it out the traditional way, but I can be here for you on occasion. If that's what you want. Adam likes you.' She pouted.

'I'm happy for you.' I slipped around her and extended my hand to Adam. 'Nice to meet you.' He took it in both of his.

'*Encantado*,' he said as he brought the palm of my hand up to his lips. His riposte and the crinkle of skin around his eyes showed that he appreciated the irony of our farewell. Then he pulled a business card from his

35

robe pocket and tucked it into my pants pocket. 'So you can contact me if you change your mind or if you have need of *anything*.' His eyes tried to snare mine, the end of his lips curved upwards.

I nodded, refusing the connection, and extracted my hand from his. He shrugged in the European way as I made my way to and through the door without even looking back at Lira.

Once I had exited the elevator and walked the length of the red carpet to the main entrance, I dropped the card into an ornate stone ashtray that stood next to the doorman's post. The uniform-clad black man hastily tossed and crushed the burning butt of his cigarette beneath the toe of his patent-leather shoe. He smiled up at me, but his eyes were weary beneath the hard lip of his military-styled cap. 'Good evening, ma'm,' he said as his hand rose to the brim of his hat and he tipped it up without it ever leaving his head. I smiled back and asked him to hail me a cab. A shrill whistle and a yellow cab appeared at the curb just as the pewter sky began to lighten. I slid a couple of dollars into the brown palm that held open the door before settling comfortably onto the cracked faux-leather seat.

Bride to Be
Izzy French

'Tighter,' Juliette said.

Sophie pulled, tugged on the ribbon and tied a bow. The stays had created a tiny waist for Juliette and the effect was stunning. They stood next to each other, the two women, the mirror confirming Juliette's silhouette. It was a true hourglass. The burgundy crushed velvet of the gothic dress fell in waves over her hips. Her breasts were just contained by the bodice. Juliette twisted left then right, smoothing the fabric over her stomach. She gave a tiny smile; knowing, self-aware, pleased with how she looked. She turned to Sophie, who could feel the heat of the other woman's breath on her cheek.

'Tighter still.'

Sophie undid the bow and tugged again, pressing her knee into Juliette's back, unsure how much tinier she could force her waist to be. But Sophie was acquiescent;

aware women like Juliette were her customers. They employed her. She remained in the shadows. They came to her because it was their time, their big day ahead. Their expectations were that she could transform them. She had an excellent reputation and her job was to help them feel wonderful. And it was a job she loved. Women were her forte. Some allowed her to caress them, making them feel special, and she felt tantalised by these brides to be, their skin glowing, their eyes shining. Some were naïve, others much more knowing. Rarely did she feel able to take things further. She had to save that for herself, or in the clubs, sweaty and hot. Not the most conducive environment for a woman with her needs.

This was the final fitting, and also the last appointment of the day. The front door was locked; their outlines would only be faintly visible through the frosted windows. Sophie was jaded, her eyes sore from concentrating on details. Once Juliette left her studio she would never see her again. They would revert to being strangers. She was going to lose her. Sophie felt a dull ache around her heart. And moistness between her thighs. She had been drawn to Juliette from the moment she stepped through the studio door, breathless, all in black.

'I want something dark,' she'd said, throwing her bag to the floor. 'Something gothic.' And Sophie had agreed. It would suit her. She suggested purple first, then they settled on a deep burgundy. The colour and fabric were beautiful. The dress had taken her many hours to create; she'd hand-worked much of it, and she was delighted with the result. She knew Juliette would be too.

Juliette's skin was pale under the lights. Sophie gazed at the space where Juliette's breasts met, pushed together, two semi-circles of delicious-looking flesh. A big jet crucifix nestled there too. She wanted to be as close as the crucifix; she was desperate to touch, to taste and to bury her head right in that spot. Probably not appropriate feelings to have about a bride to be, but not uncommon ones for her either. She wasn't going to deny them. Her body wouldn't allow that. It was an instinctive response. She would satisfy herself later, with memories, once Juliette had left. When she was alone.

Sophie was adept at holding images firmly in place in her mind, able to retrieve them for her own satisfaction. They might be glimpses, of a woman behind a carelessly pulled curtain in her changing room, of a smooth back, a softly rounded belly and pert breasts. A woman excited about her future, quick to bare her body for the designer. Anticipating her special day. All of these days were special for Sophie, and never more so than with Juliette as a customer.

'Perfect,' Juliette said, touching Sophie's bare arm.

'Almost done,' Sophie whispered, holding Juliette's hand in place, just for a moment. She would have been happy for this task to continue all night. Adjusting

Juliette's wedding dress to ensure a perfect fit. She drew away and sat cross-legged on the floor, checking the hem.

'He will love it,' Juliette said. 'Releasing me at the end of the day, thinking I'm his.'

'I have no doubt,' Sophie replied. 'The dress is beautiful, and so are you. I hope he's worth it.'

Sophie struggled to keep the bitter tone from her voice.

Juliette momentarily looked surprised, then made a face.

'Maybe, I'm not sure,' she said. Whether she meant about her beauty or his worth was uncertain. Sophie was always astonished at the doubts women brought to her studio. The imperfections they saw in their bodies, faces, hair. Sophie was blind to most of them, but then she had always been a great lover of the female form, in all its variety. Her job suited her so much. She was successful, could afford to be discerning about the brides she created dresses for.

'And I will never belong to him. I'm my own woman; no one else has done enough to earn me. Not yet.'

This sounded like a warning shot. Juliette turned to face Sophie.

'What would you think? Would you be pleased?'

She knows, Sophie thought, but that was no great surprise. Her sexuality was no dark secret. She didn't answer but lowered her head, not wishing Juliette to see her flush. With embarrassment or desire? Or a mixture of the two.

'Do you think it needs adjusting here?'

Juliette indicated the bodice. Sophie had embroidered a row of seed-pearls at the edge, entwined with intricate gold thread. Juliette was tucking her fingers between the dress and her body. The bodice was low, encasing her breasts, just, giving a medieval appearance to her overall look. Her dark nipples were just tucked below the edge. On the day she would wear a shawl of gold chiffon, but now her arms, shoulders and cleavage were on show.

'I'll check for you,' Sophie said. The stays were as tight as she could pull them. And the dress was snug at the back. It would stay in place.

'It's here, at the front, look.'

Juliette turned to face Sophie.

Sophie smoothed down the front of the bodice, making invisible adjustments, knowing from experience it was perfect. She ran her fingers along the line of pearls, feeling the warmth of Juliette's body beneath. She ran her hands down her sides. The fit was just right. She left them in place on her waist, unwilling to let go.

'You want me, don't you?' Juliette asked her. 'Like he does. Bitch. Taking advantage of the situation. Touching me.' She pulled away from Sophie, held her hands across her breasts.

Sophie looked away, uncertain how to answer, surprised at Juliette's tone. She had misread this situation, for the first time ever. Of course she wanted her. Had done since she'd entered the studio three months ago. Wanted her every time she came for a fitting, felt like she knew every inch of her body, but desperately desired intimacy with her. And she had felt some reciprocation at times. Some small flirtations – smiles, unnecessary baring of flesh, touches. They had all been signs, almost invitations to Sophie. But she had always remained aware the other woman was about to marry. Over the months Juliette had told her much about Matt. Women tended to. Like a hairdresser, people confided in her. Slowly revealed details about their lives. Told her how they liked to be fucked. About their first time with their husbands to be. Shy at first, they soon opened up, and Sophie encouraged it. She had no desire to be fucked by a man again, but hearing about other women's pleasure turned her on. She took a deep breath. It was her turn to confide. If she didn't take this chance this woman would be lost to her for ever.

'I do. But I'm not taking advantage of you. Look, hands off.' She took her hands from her waist and held them in the air. The irony of the words she used wasn't lost on either of them. She smiled.

'I'm teasing you.' Juliette returned her smile. 'It's his favourite fantasy, you know, seeing me with another woman. I've never fulfilled it for him. Although I've fulfilled many others.'

'Indeed?' Sophie feigned surprise. But she could always tell. Some women exuded innocence; some spoke of their virginity with pride, although very few did these days. Juliette was not one of those women.

Juliette touched Sophie's arm again, causing her to shudder. Her hands had encircled the other woman's waist, like his would do on the day. She tried to suppress her jealousy, to no avail.

'Yes, I've gone along with many things. But not that. You don't think I'm going to try it now, do you? Without him here to watch?'

Sophie looked away. The woman was taunting her, playing with her. But that didn't quell her desire, it intensified it.

'I don't know. I would, but then I know I'm good. Better than many men. I understand what pleases women. But if you're not interested, then that's your loss. I can find my pleasure elsewhere. You're not the only woman in the world.' This last statement felt insincere. Juliette was clearly not the only woman in the world, but she was the woman Sophie was most desperate to fuck and be fucked by.

Juliette hesitated, then leant towards her, tilting her head slightly, and kissed her. She broke away for a second.

'I think you may have helped me change my mind. I like someone strong and persuasive. It's sexy.'

Sophie could taste mint and lip gloss. She might have won her over. Juliette kissed her again. Sophie closed her eyes, imagining that this would soon end and she would be alone. But the kiss became more intense. Juliette parted her lips with her tongue, flicking around inside Sophie's mouth, twisting around her own tongue. She responded, returning the kiss. Juliette cupped her face in her hands, stroking her cheek, pushing her hair back. Sophie savoured the moment, not knowing if it would end abruptly. Juliette could change her mind, feel she had made a mistake, pay for her dress, disappear from her studio and her life. She had to seize this moment. She reached round the tiny waist and undid the bow, slowly releasing the stays, loosening the bodice. She felt Juliette's body relax. She stroked her back. Her tailor's hand had a sensitive touch. Juliette shivered, pulling back from the kiss. Sophie held her breath. Was this it? Was it all over so fleetingly? Was the one kiss all she would have to fantasise about?

'Are you sure you want me?' Juliette asked, tracing her fingers down Sophie's cheek. Sophie knew she must take her chance.

'Yes,' she whispered. Her hands released Juliette's breasts from the dress, she bent her head to the dark nipples, taking one then the other between her lips, her teeth, sucking, biting, licking, showing Juliette how she wanted her. Her breasts were full, round, soft. The skin was smooth. Sophie knew their shape, their size, and now she was experiencing their full erotic effect. The studio lights created shadows. Sophie stood back slightly, holding Juliette's shoulders, turning her from left to right, admiring her, touching with her fingertips. Juliette's eyes closed, but Sophie knew now it was not from denial but from hunger.

There had been a shift in the dynamics between the two women in the room. A subtle shift. Sophie held the balance of power now. She was the one who could excite and tantalise. Juliette was in her sway. Sophie was no longer the obedient servant, she was the dominant one.

'Take it down.' Her voice held some force. Juliette met her gaze, then pushed the loosened dress down, exposing her waist, reddened by the tightness of the stays, her full hips, encased in a thong, then her pale thighs. The dress finally fell like a pool of blood to the floor, and she stepped away from it.

Sophie ran her hands over Juliette's belly, hips, between her thighs.

'Is this what he wants to see? Another woman touching you?'

Juliette nodded.

'I think so.'

Sophie kissed her neck, leaving tiny bite marks, moving downwards, tracing round five small tattoos. She led Juliette to the sofa and quickly shed her own clothes. She was braless, her breasts small and pert; pink nipples, in contrast to Juliette's. Her nipples stood proud with desire. She stood over Juliette, her legs straddling the seated woman, and then she lowered herself onto her lap, pressing their bodies together. Juliette groaned. Sophie wondered if she would tell Matt about this later. If they would fuck to the memory. She hoped so, liking the thought of inspiring other people's pleasure. It served to increase her own. Her sex tightened as her body writhed on Juliette's lap. The thin silky fabric separating their mounds shifted against their flesh, creating static.

'Time for these to go,' she said, pulling Juliette to her feet, tugging the tiny piece of clothing first over Juliette's hips, hearing it tear as she tugged, then over her own. She threw them across the room and watched them fall together, entangled, as she hoped their bodies would soon be. They stood face to face. Juliette's body had a belly piercing in addition to the tattoos. Her bush was trimmed and neat. Sophie's body was unadorned, smooth, tanned and shaven. They were equals now, both stripped bare, facing each other, both showing the obvious signs of desire: tight, stiffened nipples, a moist sex.

They reached for each other, their hands exploratory, moving swiftly, making discoveries, finding soft places, hidden crevices, trailing over long expanses of skin. They pressed their bodies together. They were the same height. Their nipples touched. They kissed with abandon. Sophie entwined her fingers in Juliette's bush, pushed them between the sodden lips, parting her folds, making her groan. Juliette pressed the palm of her hand against Sophie's shaven mound.

Sophie suspected Juliette had experienced women before, even though she had not fulfilled Matt's desire of performing with another woman for him. She guessed that women had satisfied a different need for Juliette. Not the need to perform, but the wish to have her desires fulfilled in a different way. Desires a man could not fulfil. Sophie understood that desire well. The craving for softness, for curves, for a woman's lips on her own. The touch of someone who knows exactly how it feels to be pleased as a woman. No man had ever given Sophie that, and she had tried with many.

'Let yourself go,' Sophie urged, pushing Juliette back onto the sofa, turning her around, so her soft, ripe arse faced her; her head was pressed down into the cushions. She cradled Juliette's arse, leaned against her, spooning her, then moved back and planted kisses on her. She reached between her thighs, plunged her fingers into Juliette's wetness, drew her hand back, licked the juices, then touched herself. Her cunt was pulsating. She rubbed her own juices over Juliette's arse, seeing it shine under the lights. Then she slapped. Juliette gave a small cry of surprise.

'Why?' she asked, sounding puzzled, but not moving. In fact she shook her arse and tipped it up, like an offering.

'Many reasons.' Sophie repeated the slap, harder this time. 'For driving me to sexual distraction and leaving it until now to allow me to take you. For being beautiful and desirable. For marrying him, so you won't be mine. And you don't fool me, you've tried this before.'

Juliette shrugged her shoulders. Sophie knew she'd have to admit all these things were true. There'd been an unspoken sexual tension between them since the first appointment, when Sophie had draped fabrics against her bare skin, seeing what suited. Juliette's naked body had come as no surprise to her; the only difference was that now they could satisfy each other.

'Who says I won't be yours? My company can be bought, but not with money, with yourself.'

Juliette turned around and lay supine on the generous sofa, her head resting on a purple velvet pillow, her legs raised and parted. She played with her breasts, rolling her nipples between her fingertips. One hand strayed down over her belly and found the dark wet space between her thighs. She was giving herself obvious pleasure. Her eyes closed and she groaned. Her hips rose from the sofa, offering Sophie the sweetest view. Juliette parted her pussy lips, opened her eyes, holding Sophie's gaze.

'Is this what you'd like, where you'd like to be?'

She thrust her fingers deep into her sex, twisting and turning, exposing herself. She slid her fingers out, licked them, wiped her wetness down her inner thighs, then plunged back in again.

Sophie watched for a few moments, then fell to her

side, stroking her, massaging her body, squeezing her breasts, touching her throat, her shoulders, her arms. Their hands met in Juliette's sex; their fingers wound round each other. And then she straddled her, pinning her to the sofa. She wanted more body contact. Their sexes met. Juliette parted Sophie's shaven lips, rubbed her fingers across her clit. Her touch was light, then more insistent, her timing perfect. Again Sophie could tell she'd had experience of pleasing other women. One of the many reasons for enjoying the body of a woman, Sophie thought, and for allowing a woman to enjoy yours in return, is the innate knowledge of how to give pleasure. What pressure is required, when to touch lightly, when firmly.

Their bodies moved in unison. Sophie rocked, Juliette bucked beneath her, her obvious pleasure provoking Sophie further. She thrust her fingers into Juliette's sex, deep and hard, uncompromising, feeling it tighten around them, and she kept up the rhythm. She closed her eyes, picturing Juliette first in the dress, a gothic princess, now naked beneath her, her lust demanding and intense.

'Turn around,' Juliette whispered, her voice hoarse. Sophie, slippery and flushed, flipped around, moving her arse close to Juliette's face, anticipatory and hopeful. With her fingers she parted Juliette's lips and flicked her tongue across the other woman's clit. She gave a delicious shudder when she felt Juliette's tongue returning

49

the favour, her touch light and slow at first, then with increasing pressure and speed, sending sparks of ecstasy deep into her core. She felt it lap against her clit, then thrust deep inside her, finding its way through the fold, swallowing her copious juices. Sophie pushed her arse back, felt some light slaps against her small buttocks. They tingled in the cool air. And then the slapping stopped, but the licking, nibbling, fingerfucking continued.

Sophie held Juliette's hips, feeling them writhe under the constraint, bucking and twisting as she worked her magic. Juliette cried with pleasure as Sophie delved into her again. They were both wild with desire and the over-whelming animalistic need to come. Sophie wanted it to be simultaneous, and as she felt herself tighten around Juliette's fingers and tongue, she made her movements more urgent, thrusting, eager, heaving. Their orgasms exploded, building to a crescendo then simultaneously tipping them over the edge, to a place where no one else existed, where it was just them and the here and now, the most intense moment. The feeling was more than physical as their sexes spasmed, their throats groaned with pure pleasure. Their minds were engaged too, succumbing to the delight. Sensuous waves overwhelmed them and eventually they laid together, wet and exhausted, Juliette's legs around Sophie.

Once they'd recovered a little they touched each other's faces, kissed, tiny bird-like kisses, tender, caressing. They brushed their fingers over each other's bodies, committing each imperfection, each freckle, to the memory of their hands. So next time, and Sophie was confident there would be a next time, they would be more practised, more confident. Juliette pinched Sophie's nipples, causing them to tingle with the sweetest pain, showing little mercy as Sophie cried and gasped with the intensity of the sensation. She loved her breasts being played with, teased, sucked on, bitten. And Juliette, instinctively, obliged.

Sophie engaged all her senses, taking in her scent, vanilla, jasmine, sweet and powerful. She listened to her moan, quietly now, coming down from the high of her orgasm, enjoying the exquisite sensation of their bodies working in tandem to extend their pleasure.

'I must go, he's expecting me,' Juliette said. Reluctantly Sophie untangled herself from Juliette's warmth.

They helped dress one another, a tender moment after the fervent action that had gone before. Juliette's clothes were much more mundane than the wedding dress. A tight sweater, short skirt and boots. She ignored the thong still entwined with Sophie's in the corner of the room. She helped Sophie pull her T-shirt over her head, brushing her hands over her still tender breasts.

'Kiss me before I go,' she pleaded, and Sophie obliged, thrusting her tongue deep into Juliette's mouth, running her hand along Juliette's thigh, feeling their mingled juices between her lips. She wanted to fuck her again. Quickly this time. So she began flicking her fingers across Juliette's clit. He could wait. The other woman looked surprised, but parted her thighs obligingly, allowing Sophie access. Sophie soon elicited the now familiar groans of pleasure as she fingerfucked her, alternating between her vagina and clit, feeling the spasms build until she threw her head back and cried. And came. Quick and hard this time, not drawn-out and sensuous like last time.

'You're good,' Juliette said. 'The best. And I owe you one.'

Sophie smiled, flattered. Finally, she had to let her go, although she had no wish to. She would have liked to continue right through the night, pleasuring her and being pleasured in return. They had only just begun; there was so much mutual exploring to undertake. Juliette had demonstrated an adventurous side, and Sophie was sure she could push her boundaries further. Juliette had a licentiousness about which it was worth discovering more. Sophie could imagine introducing props. Just glancing round the room told her there was fabric for a blindfold, restraints. There were so many games they could play together.

'Will you tell him?'

Juliette shrugged. Sophie thought she would, but maybe not immediately. There was too much at stake in their immediate future. And it would never happen with him. Sophie wouldn't allow it to be spoiled in that way. It wasn't a show for a horny straight man; it was about their pleasure, their desire, not for an audience. She could imagine Juliette teasing him with the knowledge, turning him on with a slow revelation of the details.

Juliette took the proffered wedding dress, encased in a protective covering, paid and made for the door. Before disappearing into the darkness she turned to Sophie.

'Come to the wedding,' she demanded.

Sophie was silent, giving her answer some consideration. She realised she had misjudged Juliette. It was the first time she had ever felt wrong-footed by a woman. The balance of power had shifted again. She wasn't the one in control, after all. She had had to relinquish herself. And she would do so again. Juliette had played a clever game. Sophie admired her for that.

'Yes,' she replied at last, confident and happy now that this would not be their last encounter. And next time she would be fucking a married woman. Illicit sex was the best kind, in her eyes. A frisson of excitement jolted her to life again. This one could be for keeps.

Bump and Spike
Cammy May Hunnicutt

I was getting a very definite feeling about where things stood and where they might go. Fresh out of the shower with a towel around my hair and a shortie kimono robe tied around my waist, looking at Luz in a tight bikini still sweaty from our hard afternoon of beach volleyball up by the Santa Monica pier. I was feeling it more strongly every minute, even though it kind of freaked me out. I blurted it out though: 'Hey, how about you do me a favour?'

She gave me this semi-positive shrug, wide black eyes locked in on me, standing by my beat-up couch with her hip cocked like that. So I said, 'Take off your top a minute. I want to see about something.'

She kept her eyes locked on mine but crossed her arms, grabbed the tight elastic bottom of her sports bra and pulled it over her head in one movement. She stood there with it dangling from her hand, both fists on her hips, staring at me. I walked over, right up to her. And it was just like I figured: standing flat-footed with my knees straight, my mouth lined up at exactly the same height from the ground as her big black olive nipples.

I couldn't quite believe what I was doing, really. I was thinking: Damn, Cam, you can't lay this one off on 'just fooling around' or 'getting drunk and kissy with a buddy'. You're walking right up on her and jumping it off like the stone-cold dyke everybody thinks all us jocks are, anyway.

Which is what Luz was, as it turned out: straight-up. She was a born lesbian and made no bones about it. One thing I liked about your 'committed lez' was a sort of male mode. She took things in hand, knew exactly what she wanted to do and how to get optimum results. But she hadn't made a move, had she? It had all been my idea. Later she explained it, said, 'Hey, now, I don't wanna play nothing that somebody don't want to.' But my experience was, once you let her know you wanted to, look out. .

And in case she hadn't already noticed that I was down for it, I moved forward that crucial extra few inches and her big, plump right nip just slipped right between my lips. And did it ever feel good. Little salty taste, little girl taste, just the right size and shape for a pretty hungry kiss. I caressed it a little, lolled it around with my tongue and sucked it fully erect and hard. She made no move to stop me. But no move to help out, either.

I leaned back, releasing the nipple to rise and fall with her breath, shining with my saliva, and said, 'Yeah, that's what I thought.'

She looked down at me, almost a head taller, no hint of smile or emotion in her face, and said, 'That's what I was thinking, too.'

* * *

I first saw Luz on the beach between Venice and Santa Monica. Hard to miss her, really. She was the tallest girl in the group of volleyball players I'd homed in on, maybe the biggest on that stretch of sand. And not stringbean tall, either; she was solid and muscular, looked like a caramel version of Serena Williams, but way prettier. And taller. Had a knife cut across the side of her stomach and left hip. We shared an attitude, you might say. And it turned out we shared more than that.

She wasn't just prettier than the Williams' sisters; she was prettier than Jesus, in my book. She had these big, soft, dark eyes with a little uptilt at the corner, curvy eyebrows like wet paint, lush lips she always kept painted hot red. She wore her hair short, but longer in front, so it hung down like raven wings framing her face. Strong jaw, high cheekbones. Anytime she smiled at me, like after I'd dug some rogue smash out of the sand and popped it up where she could unwind on it and drive it into somebody's face like a dive bomber, her face lit up with bronze beauty.

And let me just mention that she was built like a billion pesos. The whole enchilada. She had legs all the way up, and tits that would flag down a runaway freight. Out there bounding around like a gazelle or antelope, wearing a bikini that barely did the job, light coat of sweat with grains of sugary sand falling off it, cappuccino complexion all over. She was all that and a half. Once I'd convinced the v'ball gang that I might be short and cute and white but I could hold up my end, she and I teamed up a lot.

Not surprising my life had made some major changes when I moved to California, and that a lot of it had to do with the beach. I'd been on beaches on the Mississippi 'Redneck Riviera' and the Mediterranean, of course; but living in Venice Beach was a whole bigger picture, kind of the major leagues for beach bumming. Especially since it turned out the beach was a sports arena. I was blown away by that. I saw the guys pumping iron in their little fenced-in buff-up stalag, and was down at the basketball courts on Ocean Front the first day I moved in. But what was new and exciting to me was what was going on right out on the sand. Over The Line was cool enough, playing softball on the sand with no mitts or mound or battery. Made me wish I'd gone to school out there in Santa Monica or Manhattan Beach. But what really got me going was beach volleyball. Right away I noticed those big golden chicks playing two on two. And the more I learned about it, the more excited I got. This was a professional sport, with a tour! Unbelievable, really; the college teams with the gyms and uniforms and coaches and expensive hardwood floors were the amateurs while the pros were out there playing on sand in their bathing suits. Two on two. Stripped down, zero-defects face-off. Amazing.

Quite a sight, too. A bunch of slim, strong women in tiny bikinis out there moving like oiled kangaroos. Jumping, diving, uncurling on a ball to slam it into somebody's face. One hot, sexy, wet, electric event.

I hadn't really played v'ball before, other than rainy days in the high-school gym. Boondocks Mississippi not being quite the hotbed of volleyball that California beaches are. But I picked it up super-quick. It's usually a fairly quick transition for basketball hotshots like myself and after a couple of weeks being down there all afternoon I was getting on the courts and winning a little grudging respect. I would have loved to play the pro circuit. I was really in the prime of my ability and had no real outlet for it. But there was the same curse that kept me out of basketball past high school: I was just too damned short. That made twice I'd been shafted by being 'petite'.

But I was good enough for the local level. I could jump pretty well and, even if I couldn't sail up and block a spike by one of those six-two goddesses, I could move faster and had quick hands. It's not just rocketing the ball over the net that gets the point, it's making it land in the sand. And I could dig a slam out of a gopher's butt. The bunch I fell in with were mostly kind of street girls. No college experience, but lots of beach ball time. There were a couple who'd played at UCLA, but the ones I hung with were mostly Chicana *chicas* who I gathered had managed to get away from the whole *cholo*, gang-banger scene. Some very tough gals, let me tell you; came up playing handball on doper park walls with ex-cons sporting whole buckets of teardrop tattoos. Girls with combat decorations and some god-awful tats in messed-up places. Unpolished, 'street' style of play. We'd cruise down the boardwalk and shoot some baskets, too. I was giving them some roundball tips, which they didn't take to at first, but came to appreciate. They'd never really had any decent coaching. But they were some scary v'ball vixens.

After a while Luz fell into siding with me and we made a great team. She'd be the top end, soaring around up there, keeping the net clear, pounding spikes down right over people, just sort of generally Sky Captain And The World Of Booyah. Meanwhile, I'd be Ms Bottom Line, scampering around underneath, digging them out, serving them up, bumping them right into her fist coming down on them like Thor's hammer. We used to draw crowds out there, volley dollies and their dewds sitting on folder chairs and chill chests, cyclists and skaters stopping to check us out. Our high level of play, but also our high level of Babe. Two very hot chicks: short, golden blonde lingerie model and big brown brawler looking like Hustler meets American Gladiators meets American Me. We sent a lot of dynamic duos off the court with whupped butts, and a lot of beachboy hipsters home with a stiffy in their designer Lycra shorts.

We got to be pretty tight. I ran with her and Gabi and a couple of the other volleygirls, typical jockette drinks-after-games sort of thing, but Luz was kind of a special friend. We used to talk a lot, sipping shots at Danny's or The World or coffee at The Sidewalk Café. Telling me about banging in Echo Park, listening to me talk about modelling, about Paris and Majorca. She would drop by my place a lot after playing, since I lived close to the boardwalk. Grab a shower and change, maybe have a drink or two, listen to K-Earth or the WIZ and shoot the shit. Not the usual girl-talk. Neither one of us was much into chatting about guys or clothes. She came from a family of low-riders and was one of the few girls I ever found worth talking to about cars.

Then one time we were sitting around, listening to some Rickie Lee Jones mp3's I just picked up, savouring some decent Sauza tequila. She was lounging on my distressed sofa, still wearing her suit from the beach, sweaty around the crotch and top of the bra, me still wet from the shower. I was leaning back in a folding chair with my feet on my rickety dinner table. I had my hair in the towel and she was sitting there combing her hair dry with her fingers. We got to talking about modelling, body types. She thought it was amazing that you could earn good money just by being a size, every measurement on your body being exactly a perfect size six or whatever. Even a perfect half-size.

I told her I was too short for runway work and she was too tall. But she might well make some money showing lingerie, which was of interest to her because she had no education and had trouble finding good work. What I was really thinking she should do was get on down to Star Strip and shimmy her glorious bare ass up the pole to Big Tips Land. But she has all this Catholic family weirdness, like half the barrio. She said she'd think about it then stood up and said, 'Think I need a shower?'

I said, 'I was going to suggest it. Or breaking out the air freshener.'

I got up too, to fetch her a fresh towel, but there was something about the way she just stood there, nothing moving, like a mahogany statue wrapped in two damp, sandy strips of lipstick-red swimsuit. I was thinking: *Sports Illustrated* should get a load of this. But then I kind of stopped thinking. And ended up standing there with a big hard nipple in my mouth and my robe starting to feel too constrictive.

Which is what I was telling you about, me coming on to this big bad banger *chola* with knife scars and a Virgin of Guadalupe tattoo. Which had me in a state, make no mistake about that. Conflicting emotions, as they say. But the main one was, I was getting really, major-league excited about it. Luz was one dominant, awesome piece of work all over. Even if you never saw her move, which was like out-takes from an *Animal Planet* special on predators. She could dominate your ass while passed out. Standing there, looming over me like a dark urge, she threw my mind into neutral, maybe even park. Her tits were good-sized, but mostly they just looked strong. Like something clenched and powerful. With those purple-plum nipples out there, moving around with her every breath or flex. Riding high and regal on a fluted ribcage with no hint of give. And draping down off the bottom of those cathedral ribs were rows of taut, cut-up abs like a six-pack of butterscotch muffins slowly rising in an oven. And at the bottom of that was her mound.

I mean you hear that term *mons veneris*, and all that, but hers actually was: big and hard as a Golden Delicious apple, swelling luxuriantly up on her pelvic girdle, sparse silky black hair lying plastered down on it like wet feathers. And what it curled down to was a round dimple you could have set a pencil in, just the tip where two puffy lips came together before gliding down and around between two slim but heavily muscled thighs. Topping graceful calves built for propelling her a yard off the sand anytime it seemed necessary. You could stare at her all day and just sort of lock up because anything you were looking at was screaming out an invitation to stroke it with your fingers. Better yet, your lips. But where would you start?

She solved that one easy enough; snaked out two long, businesslike arms and set her wrists on my shoulders. She spread her fingers and knitted them in a quick motion, almost clicking together behind my neck. I'm not easy to intimidate, but this girl could likely do the trick if she felt like it. But that wasn't what she felt like, it seemed. Barely audibly, she said, 'Shake your head, *güera*.'

I saw what she meant and gave my hair a shake, kind of lashing it out, flinging the towel off and letting my goldilocks tumble down on her hands. She leaned down and nuzzled it, eyeing it close up, sniffing it deeply. She said, 'Looks like I get to bring home the gold, *verdad*?'

I said, 'Well, if you ask nice.'

She smiled. She had a really sweet smile, actually. Then she cupped my downy nape with one hand and used the other one to give my kimono belt a sharp tug and slide through the curtains to cup my damp towheaded curlies in her hand. She rotated her long, strong fingers a little, kind of smearing my labia around, and must have noticed I was already damned wet, so she flicked a big finger inside, just kind of lying there. Then curling it, joint by joint, dragging her nail along some mighty slick real estate until it plunked right into me. I did this kind of sigh and she did a couple of slow in-outs, then pulled it out and brought it up between our faces. She moved the wet tip close to my mouth and I pursed my lips. She slid it in, let me taste myself, then pulled it out and into her own mouth, kind of slurping on it. She gave me another grin and said, 'That nice enough for you, *chula*?'

I said, 'You've done this before, huh?'

She gave me this feral grin and stroked her hand up into my hair. I said,

'Lemme give it a shot, here.'

I did the same move. See one, play one, my grandaddy always said when we played cribbage. I'd been dying to pet her puss, anyway, stroke that prominent mound. She filled my cupped hand nicely. Perfectly. Just a warm, puffy handful of caramel-cream Chicana pussy, pulsing as I squeezed. I could feel her lips opening and closing under my fingers, pulsing like a clam. I copied her finger insertion, teasing her with a long, slow drag up between her sloppy-wet lips, then circling around at the opening a little before slipping inside her. None of that tight virginal business with our Luz. No way. She was a big girl, with a big pussy, and it was wide, wet and wild. I gave it three fingers and started pumping them in and out, bracing the heel of my hand in the sparse Indian hair that decorated that big soft mound. I was getting more thrilled by the minute.

Not as much as her, though. Her eyes narrowed down until they were all black, no sign of white around the irises. Her nostrils flared and quivered. Her lips pulled back, baring her big, squarish teeth. I could see up into her mouth, hear her panting like an overheated hound dog. Tell you the truth, she was downright scary. I'm no kind of chicken, you all know, and I can handle the rough stuff whether it's on the field or the mattress, but I was getting the feeling I was cranking up some big monster machine I couldn't even begin to control. She was shuddering, gasping and gripping my shoulders so hard that her fingers felt like wood. All that on top of her size and strength gave me the feeling I was in for one wild ride. So I moved it out another notch: slipped my whole hand in her, slopping into that big dripping pipeline while grinding the heel of my palm onto her clit.

All of a sudden she slipped some sort of cog inside that big Aztec head of hers and I lost any sense of having any say in the situation. She whipped her head back and gave this howl like some sort of mariachi wolf, then bobbed back down, bumped her forehead on mine and nuzzled my hair. I leaned my head back, continuing to slam my hand up in her, and slid my lips around to hers. She crushed her mouth on mine, as much teeth as lips, and ran her tongue halfway down to my gizzard. She was gasping, kind of inhaling me and I was just as into it, one hand on her tit kneading her nipple between two fingers, and the other one hammering up inside her. Being shorter was working to my advantage. Well, her advantage, too, because I had a good angle to get up in there. And hang on, because she was starting to vibrate around like she was having a *grande mala* seizure. Her whole body pushed up against me, throbbing. Clenching. I thought she was going to crush my hand flat, her pussy was grinding on it so bad. Then all of a sudden she came.

I felt this flood of hot fluid on my hand, running out on my wrist and forearm, and she crunched down on me like a big vice made out of sirloin. She reached up and grabbed my head with both hands, holding it while she tongue-fucked my mouth, and I could feel the pulsing contractions in her washboard abs. I thought she was going to shake herself apart, right on top of me. She slid her mouth off mine and around into the hair on the side of my head. She started kissing my hair and kind of chewing on it. Then she went limp on me. I held her up with one hand on her big hard tit and the other buried in her gushing pussy, but she was heavy and giving me a hard time. She pulled her head away and stared down at me a minute, started babbling something in really fast

Spanish. Then her eyes kind of swam back into focus and she grabbed me.

Her massive orgasm hadn't cooled her off any, and definitely hadn't weakened her. She leaned her head down onto my shoulder, lips stroking my neck, and cupped my bush with one hand, gripping the front hoop of my pubic bone with fingertips pushed inside me. The other hand nabbed my left tit and squeezed on it, hard. Which was fine with me. She'd given me a taste of something and now it looked like she was hitting me with the full course. She backed me up against the wall, shoving me ahead of her while kneading and mashing me with both hands. I have been in the clutches of some pretty big, strong, determined men in my time, let me tell you. But there was something even more controlling about Luz, something relentless and implacable. She rolled up on me like a TAC squad, booking no alibis. I found it even easier to just let myself go, just fall into her hands and go along for the ride. That's not easy for me to do, but I like it when I can, because it opens you up for a lot more, and fuller, pleasure. Which was going down right then and there, was the message I was getting. I had a feeling this was going to be one of those life landmark situations, and was I ever right about that. *Yowsuh.*

I was backing up, just kind of buried under her pressure on me. I couldn't really figure out what to do. I put my hands on her tits, which filled them up and spilled over, and that seemed to work. I caught her nipples right in my palms and started rolling them around while I squeezed. She growled and grabbed my crotch harder. Her hand filled up the 'notch' between my thighs, my suddenly very damp pussy lips sitting on her fingers as she pressed up, like she was lifting me off the floor. Her other hand had moved across to my other tit and was massaging it in a driving pulse that was getting me very hot and fuzzy. Then my ass hit the wall and I was trapped, surrounded by hot, sweaty brown skin and the smell of a groin that had been working up a sweat for hours without washing it off and now was oozing musk and girl jizz.

I had my eyes closed, my head lolling back, just wiped out by her fingers wriggling inside me and her thumb strumming my clit. Then she slowly bent her fingers, raked a nail across my G spot and stroked her thumb pad down my button. I realised she was making a fist. And moving it back and forth inside me, like a big piston. A large fist, too, pushing into me like she was trying to find the back door. That was kind of a novelty for me, and I adjusted myself to letting it happen. She'd crouched down, almost kneeling, staring at my patch of goldenrod pubies while she worked in and out, burying her wrist out of sight. I stared down, too, held against the wall by her spread hand on my tit, pushing and kneading in time with her fisting. My nipple was popping in and out from under a finger, getting a dull tickle while my

68

pussy got stroked and stretched. I bent my knees, lifted my feet onto her thighs for support, tilting my pelvis to allow her to slug it into me harder.

Suddenly the locomotive stroke of her fist inside me stopped. She fanned her fingers around inside me, brushing my G spot and a few other spots that probably have letters, too. She looked up into my eyes and clenched her fist again. It felt like she'd grabbed a handful of my insides. She was panting like a dog, her eyes wild, her nostrils dilated and pulsing with quick breaths. She was beautiful, wild and savage. I tried to lean forward, kiss her. I brought my hands up to her shoulders, held the sides of her neck, tried to pull her face to me. I couldn't budge her. She stood up out of her crouch, my feet slipping off her legs. But they didn't reach the floor. She was holding me off the ground, pinioned by her hand on my tit, hoisted by her hand inside me. That alone stimulated me into some deep quivers that I felt against her curled fingers. My head fell forward, but she moved her hand off my breast and under my chin to hold me up where we could look each other in the face.

Slowly, she curled her arm. I was being lifted by her fist inside me, sliding up the wall as she raised her arm with me speared on it. She moved her forearm under my jaw as she lifted me, rotating her wrist back and forth to keep me buzzing down there.

OK, I was a newbie to this whole level of things, but

I don't mind saying my mind was pretty much blown. If you'd asked me, I would have said it would have been impossible to jam a whole big old fist up my snatch, much less a bunch of wrist and forearm. I definitely would have said it was impossible to lift me off the floor by nothing more than my pussy.

On the other hand, I'd been playing beach ball with Luz for six months and seen her do quite a bit of impossible shit. For that matter, I'd been known to pull off a few things in my own athletic career that defied the Laws of WTF.

She was prodding up into me, jabbing her fist up and stopping. I'd kind of toss up off her arm, then fall back down while she growled and groaned like a wrestler. She slid her hand up from my boob and stroked along my collarbone, pushing her forearm under my chin, up against my throat. I was staring into her eyes, but they were a little vacant. She was wild-eyed and wanton, is what she was, grunting like a boxer as she fisted me silly. She leaned in on her forearm, lips opening and closing like she was saying a rosary. I clenched my throat muscles, like I was hanging off her arm. And just that amount of leverage left her arm free enough of my weight to start to really pound me to pieces in a big way. She was jerking it out, then throwing it back in like a right hook, swinging from the knees, slamming into me. My pussy lips were stretched around her lower arm, sopping wet

70

as they slid along her skin as it punched and out. She was into a solid tempo, steady beat of her fist into my inner chambers, leaning harder against me. Her forearm starting to cut off my air, the blood to my brain. I was becoming light-headed, things getting a little dark at the edges. I was a hair away from passing out, getting a buzz on the asphyxia, now that I look back on it.

But more so from the huge, hard socketing into me of her muscular fist and wrist. It was making a sucking, hydraulic sort of sound, squishing in and out, a splattery sound. Over which she was growling and muttering and gnashing her teeth. Yipping out a few Mexican *ay, ay, yi*'s. I was barely with the programme any more, hanging there broiling in ecstasy, but also nodding out on her, everything fading from my vision, replaced by that slurping, thudding, star-studded super-fucking of her jackhammering fist. Thor's hammer, right up my ying-yang. I was just about gone, I don't know which way. The lack of breath and blood was intensifying everything. Suddenly she screamed something inarticulate and pulled her arm away from my throat and rammed her hand straight up in the air. I rode up almost to the ceiling, hoisted on her fist. Air whooshed in, my carotids blared blood to my reeling brain. I came with a thermonuclear whoosh, honey. I felt the top of my head blow off from a mushroom cloud and my hands and legs flap around like seal flippers. I just hung there and shook, looking down into Luz's face, which was hard and

71

commanding and severe. And another orgasm landed on me like a building falling down. That was pretty much the end of Cammy, as I knew her. Side out.

I flopped down and she dropped to her knees, lowering her arm. I fell on her in a fireman's carry position, draped over her shoulder and twitching and tossing. I felt her come, too, a contact high. She knelt on my rug with me hanging over her while we vibrated and whinnied.

* * *

I couldn't tell you how we ended up on the bed. But at some point I was breathing normal, thinking normal, feeling normal except for being kind of buffed-up all over, lax and lazy, seeing the dim insides of my bedroom through a soft cloud like looking through peach-coloured nylon stocking while up to my ears in a hot tub full of champagne. I was lying there all spread-eagled and wide open, with my head on Luz's arm and one leg draped over hers. She was kind of snoozing, too, but when I turned to look at her she opened those big eyes and fixed her dark gaze on me, just a slight smile. Waiting to hear from me.

I just lay there looking at her for a while. Nothing that happened in the past hour had made her look any less fabulous and precious. *Au contraire*. She reached her other arm across, lolling her breasts over her ribs, and took my hand in hers. Brought it up to her lips and gave me a long, slow kiss on the back of it, then moved it down to lie between her legs and moved so her thighs kind of clamped it in position. Just that, nothing else. Just an endearment, I guess you'd say. I was starting to see her as not a hard case all the way down, like most folks would think of her. And me, too.

I kind of blurted it out to her, without thinking. 'Listen, Luz. You're a total lesbian, right? All girl, all the time?'

She smiled and gave my hand a quick squeeze with her big, toned thighs. 'Where'd you get that idea, *querida*?'

'Well, I mean ...' I didn't know quite what I meant. 'So how about me? What does this make me?'

'*Hijole*! I get your cherry?'

'Well, I've been with some girls before. But not like that. Not like this.'

'So you're afraid you're all queer and shit?'

'OK, yeah.' I don't know if 'afraid' was quite the word, but it was kind of disturbing.

'And you're thinking it's a bad thing.'

'Well, I wouldn't go that far.' She chuckled and gave my hand another squeeze. 'But, you know ... It's not how I'd see myself.'

'You could see yourself the way I'm seeing you right now, might not seem so bad.'

'Oh, it's great, babe. We're a hell of a team. I guess ...' I thought it over a little, feeling her thighs constricting and releasing my hand with each breath. 'It's such a stereotype. Here's the tough tomboy jock, and oh, guess what, she's a dyke.'

She lay there looking at me, silent. Not uncomfortable at all. I still had a glow on, couldn't have been uncomfortable if I'd wanted to. Then she rolled towards me a little, scooted her ass back a little bit and said, 'Look here, girlfriend.'

I looked. Lordy, she was a smasher. Half backlit by streetlights through the window, rich and dark and smooth as cinnamon chocolate, hard and firm and *picante*. She almost whispered, in this dark, smoky voice, 'Like what you're looking at?'

I cut my eyes at her. What? Trick question?

She said, 'What does that make you feel like?'

I laughed out loud. 'What a body in their right mind would feel like, honeybunch. Like I want to touch, stroke, kiss. I just want to drip all over you like a coat of maple syrup. That's what you look like.'

'So what does that make you? Other than in your right mind?'

I started to say something but she said, 'How'd you like to fuck George Clooney?'

I laughed again. 'Can you hook me up?'

'See?' she said. 'Ever heard of bisexual? You feel like you been repressed? Finally creeping out of the closet, here? Sorry if I don't think you've been holding anything in. Not the type.'

I said, 'Well. OK. I don't guess it changes much to put names on it, does it? I just felt something bigger and heavier tonight. Like maybe it's more real for me.'

She laughed. 'Thanks for the compliment, *güera*. I'd say you just do what you feel like, and *who* you feel like, and you'll be fine.'

I sagged down on the bed, head on her forearm, and just felt it flow over me. She had it figured, all right. I never worried about that stuff ever again. I said, 'Well, I hope you're not going to do something regrettable.'

She cocked one of those thick glossy eyebrows and I shrugged. 'You know. Like getting dressed or going home.'

She laughed her big, up from the tummy laugh, and said, 'I don't think we're done here, do you?'

I lowered my eyes like a bashful virgin and shrugged my shoulders. And wriggled my fingers against her pussy. She laughed again and curled her arm up, rolling my head right into a nice deep kiss. During which she cupped my ass to draw me up on my hip, facing her, then trailed her fingers over my hip and down to stroke my gold fur, and dip down where it was sparse and kind of slick. I grabbed her ass, too, and started stroking it, like polishing hardwood. I moved my lips off hers and around to her ear. Licked a tongue in-out, in-out, and whispered, 'I always love games with extra innings.'

She was gliding back and forth on my labia, gently

stroking and petting. That should have seemed light-weight after our previous set-to, but it felt great. I kissed her ear and moaned lightly. She whispered, '*Eso, cariño, eso.*' My eyes were closed and I felt like drifting away as she slid her hand back and forth on my moistening lips. Back and forth.

Then one finger dropped down from the others and parted my lips like the prow of a ship, sliding back and forth inside, slipping through the slick wet like a dolphin. I gripped her ass cheek for dear life, drew my other hand up behind her head and clenched her to me. And felt three fingers enter me, slowly plunging inside, then bending to grip and doing a little dance around the Spot of Spots. I groaned again, but couldn't help wonder if I could handle another fist-fuck so soon. My pussy was not used to anything that big and rough. I could take a punch, but had never been socked up on the inside like that.

She must have sensed my apprehension because she murmured, 'I gotcha, Blondie. Just easy does it this time.' I nodded, surrendering myself to the sensation she was spreading around inside my vagina, nibbling on the side of her throat as she stroked me fine and sleek and tender. Her fingers spread into a goblet shape, as though she was holding an orange, and rotated inside me as her thumb moved down to do a slow rhythmic pressure on my clit.

I said, 'Oh, God, Luz. That's wonderful. I could take this all night.'

She gave a wonderful nasty chuckle right by my ear and said, 'Works for me. Hey, that Clooney guy?'

I just nodded dumbly, soaking up the sensations.

'Well, here's the twist, *mami*. Men don't know dick about how to play with pussies.'

She sure did, though. Her fingers were dancing in me, doing a sexy tango on my leaking membranes while I just hung on to her and whimpered. I reached between her thighs, but couldn't really get it together to do much. She said, 'Just relax. This one's on me. Special introductory offer for first-time blonde dykes.'

I tried to laugh, but it was just too much. I was coming adrift, is what I was doing, just floating out to sea while she skimmed and massaged my cavity, always keeping that pulsing pressure on my clit, like the bass beat of some off-the-charts *salsa* number. At some point she gently rolled me over on my back, and my arms and legs fell into the sheets like loose sacks of corn. She leaned in and started tonguing my nipples, teasing a little, but mostly just giving me a good, solid coat of saliva on both tips, now and then sucking one or the other up between her soft lips for some suction and nibbling.

And all the while that backbeat on my clit. That adagio inside me, giving me chills and thrills in places I didn't even know I had places. First time I ever came with no warning. No prelude or overture, just Blam! and I was spinning off into Sparkle City freefall. I shook hard, my hips coming up off the bed, my arms and toes and fingers and probably hair all spreading and stretching out, quivering. While she laughed into my aureoles and did something with her hand in me that I can't even explain. All it did was touch off another climax right on top of the first. I was a goner. Dead cat position with probably little 'X's on my eyes and smoke pouring out of my ears.

Which she figured was a good time to pull her hand slowly out of me and trail it down the inside of my thighs. Drawing lines of sparks through the darkness behind my eyelids, like a rearview mirror scraping along a concrete wall at about forty miles an hour. I gasped and kind of sunfished, then felt her mouth on me. She just placed her lips on my labia, matching up like some secret sorority kiss, and moved them slowly, just a soft soul kiss on my puss that had me purring in orgasm aftershock and cooing like a bride. The more spectacular effects of my inner light show were fading into a sweet, mellow afterglow and I reached down to bury both hands in her hair. Then she flicked her tongue, just once, full against my clit, and I went off again.

* * *

Next thing I was really fully aware of, we were sprawled out side by side with my head on her shoulder and her hand loosely gripping my ass with a couple fingers snuggled into the crack. I was just lying there looking down at her body and running my hands over it a little. It was like having my own private sculpture museum and I was learning all those incredible shapes and textures by Braille. She had her nose buried in my hair and kept combing it with her fingers. She said, 'Think I could dye mine blonde?'

I couldn't believe it. 'That would be so stupid, Luz. You've got beautiful hair and it suits your colour. Why would you want to mess with that?'

She kept fondling my hair, letting it trickle through her fingers so she could see the light through it. Kind of dreamy, she said, 'Whether they admit it or not, all Mexican girls want to be blonde. Have creamy white skin and pink nipples.'

At the moment I had my hand on her hip, the colour of dark roast *café au lait*, loving the look and feel, so I said, 'You want to be white? You must be crazy.'

She smiled and twined her fingers in my hair to lift my face up to her lips. She murmured, 'That's me, *bebe* doll. Living *la vida loca*.'

The Beach House
Liz Coldwell

Aiden didn't think anyone would ever buy the beach house. It stood at the end of the headland, isolated from the rest of the homes in their little waterfront community, its weathered frontage facing out towards the vast swell of the Pacific Ocean.

Its previous owner had been some big-shot film producer, who'd wanted a weekend bolthole, away from the smoggy skies and raging stress of central Los Angeles. Though all he'd done was bring the stress with him, she reflected sourly, throwing noisy, sprawling, drug-fuelled parties, loud enough to disrupt the peace of the year-round residents. The man had been squat, self-important; it might not have been surprising that he had no interest in becoming a wider part of the community, but he never made even the most basic effort to be civil towards his neighbours. Aiden hadn't been sad when he'd been very publicly chased by the IRS for millions in unpaid taxes, and had to put the house on the market, along with properties he owned in London and New York, to help pay what he owed.

Though that had been over a year ago now, and still the place stood empty. The asking price had been lowered nearly half a million from the original figure, but Aiden couldn't remember the last time she'd even seen the realtor's station wagon driving along the main highway that ran through Minola Beach, on its way to a client viewing of the property. With the economy the way it was, a weekend retreat had become a luxury for all but the very rich, and those with money to throw around just didn't seem to be interested in this sleepy corner of Southern California.

Every morning, Aiden jogged along the path that led by the empty house, and each time it seemed a little sadder, a little more in need of repair. No one bothered to do anything more than make the odd, cursory check on the property these days. Winter was coming and, though the climate was usually temperate here, it wasn't unknown for damaging storms to hit the coast. A mean little part of her couldn't help feeling glad the producer still continued to lose money on his investment, but she'd always loved that house, and she hated to see it gradually falling apart.

But today, as she slogged along the beach and up the

zigzagging path that would take her past the beach house, listening to pounding dance music on headphones to help the four-mile route pass more quickly, her thoughts were anywhere but on the crumbling state of the old property. A friend of a friend had informed her, with purely malicious intent she was sure, that Julie and her new girlfriend were about to make their union legal. They had a civil ceremony planned in Hawaii, the place where Aiden and Julie had originally met. It had been less than six months since they'd split up; she found it almost impossible to believe her lover of nearly four years had found someone else so soon, let alone someone she apparently wanted to spend the rest of her life with. Had their time together really meant so little to Julie, that she could discard it so easily?

Aware she could slip into maudlin self-pity if her thoughts continued along this track, Aiden was brought up short by the sight of an SUV pulling to a halt in front of the beach house. The black vehicle, so sleek and shiny it could have come straight off the dealer's lot, had a couple of surfboards strapped to the roof. That sight alone was enough to pique her interest.

Stopping short of the house, Aiden watched as a woman emerged from the SUV's passenger side, pausing to take a long, critical look at the building. Her red hair fluttered in the breeze, and she pushed it away from her small, freckled face with an arm on which dozens of thin silver bracelets jangled. A moment later, she was joined by another woman, this one blonde, with bare, tanned legs emerging from a pair of faded denim shorts. The two conversed in high, excited voices; Aiden wasn't close enough to make out any of the words, but there was much giggling as the blonde tossed a key in the air and caught it again. She unlocked the door, and the two women went inside.

There didn't appear to be any sign of the realtor, but that wasn't a surprise if the two women had just taken legal possession of the key to the property. If these were her new neighbours, maybe Aiden ought to pop her head round the door and introduce herself. Maybe she could get a feel for whether these two were likely to be any friendlier than the beach house's previous owner.

She switched off her iPod and pulled the headphone buds out of her ears. Tucking a stray strand of dirty-blonde hair behind her left ear, she fixed her face in a welcoming smile. Making new friends might help go some way to softening the hurt she couldn't help but feel on hearing of Julie's impending wedding.

For the first time in months, one of the shutters covering the windows at the back of the house had been opened. As Aiden made her way up the path, she realised she had a view into one of the bedrooms. She'd expected the place to be empty inside, but it appeared the producer had left behind most of the furniture. Maybe his tax bill was so big he'd had to sell that off, too.

But it wasn't the king-sized bed with its ornate wrought-iron rails, or the huge oak armoire, that really caught her eye. A Chinese-patterned screen stood to one side of the bed, and the blonde had just stepped out from behind it. She'd discarded the denim shorts, and wore only the skimpiest pair of polka-dot-patterned panties on her lower half. The hard brown discs of her nipples jutted at the tight white T-shirt whose hem barely reached her navel, making it clear she wore no bra beneath it. Aiden found her gaze riveted to the girl's small, round breasts, any thoughts of making any kind of formal introduction wiped from her mind as the T-shirt was slowly peeled upwards and casually tossed to the floor. Naked but for the cute little panties, the girl laid herself down on the bed.

Aiden should have walked away at that moment and resumed her jog, leaving the two strangers to whatever they might be planning, but she couldn't tear her eyes from the unfolding events. With quiet, cautious steps, she crept closer to the house. The low back gate had been left latched but not locked, and she let herself inside. Later, she couldn't say what compelled her to make her way up the small path, overgrown with crabgrass, and crouch down by the bedroom window so she could see without being seen. Her libido had nosedived in the wake of her break-up with Julie; she'd had no interest in meeting another woman, and she hadn't even contemplated reaching for her vibrator to fill the void in her life. Now, it seemed a part of her she'd let fall dormant had come surging back to life, and was demanding satisfaction.

Glancing back to the bedroom action, Aiden saw the redhead was performing a strip of her own. Her elegant, body-skimming black dress couldn't have been more of a contrast to her friend's casual, beach-bunny attire, and Aiden found herself wanting to know more about the two of them. She and Julie had been so alike in so many ways, but that hadn't been enough to sustain their love; maybe these two, who seemed like such opposites on this initial viewing, had stronger foundations for their relationship.

The black dress slithered to the floor, and Aiden had to stifle a gasp of lust at the sight of the redhead's body. A cream lace bra appeared to be losing the fight to contain her luscious, full breasts, and matching panties barely covered the plump mound of her pussy. As curvaceous as her girlfriend was slender, with freckles covering the creamy upper slopes of her huge tits, the girl was the most beautiful thing Aiden could recall seeing in Minola Beach – and that included the C-list starlets who'd rolled up to so many of Mr Producer's raucous beach parties.

In an unconscious gesture, Aiden palmed her own breast. Even through the layers of her sweat top and sturdy sports bra, she could feel her nipple, pebbled and taut with desire. She tugged at it, feeling an answering jolt of desire low in her belly.

The redhead hooked her fingers in the other girl's panties, tugging them down. Aiden swore she could smell the blonde's excitement through the half-open window, briny as the neighbouring ocean.

The redhead climbed onto the bed, parted her girl-friend's thighs and pressed her mouth to the blonde's pussy. Aiden could see her head bobbing, and imagined how it would feel to have her face mashed against her own split, a sinuous little tongue lapping at the wet pink interior as she writhed and humped against her ass against the covers.

Until this moment she'd never considered herself to be a voyeur but, faced with the delicious sight of the two girls at play, she couldn't deny the strength of her feelings. Driven by an almost frantic lust, she thrust a hand down the front of her sweatpants, pushed aside the crotch of her panties and registered the dampness of the fabric.

Her finger skittered over her clit, sending tremors of pure, undiluted pleasure through her. A moan almost escaped her lips, and she bit down hard on the fleshy part of her other hand to stifle the sound. Though she doubted either woman would hear her; they were too wrapped up in each other to notice anything else. They'd rearranged themselves so that they now lay top to tail, each licking the other's sex.

A dark, envious fire burned in Aiden's body. She wished it was her pussy the redhead was laving with long sweeps of her tongue; her tits that were being caressed between slender, red-polished fingertips; her mouth that explored the soft, wet crevices of the redhead's sex. Instead, her role was that of a horny observer, playing feverishly with her own clit as the couple on the bed licked and caressed and loved each other.

The blonde came first, pulling her mouth off her girl-friend's pussy to squeal out her pleasure. Keen to return the favour, she composed herself almost at once, using her fingers to bring her lover off. Aiden couldn't quite see whether she had two or three of her digits buried deep in the redhead's hole, but they were obviously having the desired effect, because she arched her back in climax, treating Aiden to an unforgettable view of her tits straining against the cups of the bra she hadn't both-ered to remove. The sights and sounds of two women so consumed by passion had Aiden's own vagina convulsing, her juices flooding out to soak her underwear further.

She sank to the ground, wrung out by the strength of her orgasm. By the time she was able to drag herself to her knees and take a peek through the bedroom window, the two women had left the room. Hoping they had no plans to inspect the back of their property, she was instead surprised to hear the sound of a large motor vehicle driving away from the beach house at speed. When she checked, the SUV was gone. As she walked back down to the beach, she thought about their strange, speedy exit; almost as though they'd been the ones who were afraid of being caught where they shouldn't be. But she didn't pay it too much mind, more consumed with the idea of hunting out her waterproof vibrator when she got home, so she could take it into the shower with her and relive the encounter she'd just watched, over and over.

* * *

When the SUV didn't return to the beach house over the next few days, and the place showed no obvious signs of renewed habitation, Aiden realised the girls had never had any intention of buying it. They must have borrowed the key from the realtor, and simply used the property as a scene for their naughty little sex game. She couldn't blame them; she'd had one of the best experiences of her life just watching them, so what kind of thrill must they have had, fucking on a stranger's bed? Maybe they did it on a regular basis; with so many homes for sale, they could fuck in a different location every week, if they chose. From the millionaire mansions in Bel Air to – well, to a run-down but atmospheric house that overlooked an all-but-deserted beach. Aiden could just imagine the two of them feigning interest in the latest listings. She'd bet they gave false names, so they couldn't be traced if the owner came home and found his bed sheets rumpled and the room smelling of recent girl-sex. And when they handed back the key, saying regretfully that the property wasn't quite what they were looking for, the realtor would never know the truth of their intimate viewing.

And she'd have continued to believe that, if she hadn't been grocery shopping in town one afternoon and spotted a familiar figure through the plate-glass frontage of Minolta Beach Real Estate. The redhead sat at a desk by the window, making a phone call. Unable to help herself, Aiden pushed open the door and walked in. Spotting her, the redhead gestured for her to take a seat on the opposite side of the desk. As Aiden did so, she spotted a plaque next to the girl's PC, reading JAYNE HOLLANDER.

Finishing the call, the redhead turned her full attention to Aiden, fixing her with a dazzling smile. 'Hi, I'm Jayne. Thanks for choosing Minolta Beach Real Estate. How can I help you?'

Faced with the reality of the situation, Aiden didn't quite know what to say. Eventually, she stammered, 'It's about the beach house out on the headland.'

'Oh, the old Millman property. You know, you're the second enquiry we've had about it in a week. I was over there showing it just last Friday. It looks a little run down from the outside, but it's a beautiful place. A real investment. I'll just let Nancy know where we're going, and then we can pop over there so you can take a look.'

Jayne rose from her desk, and called to a woman at the back of the office. 'Nancy, I'm taking a client to the Millman house. If anyone calls, I'll be back in an hour, OK? Right, now if you'd like to follow me – I'm sorry, I didn't catch your name.'

'It's Aiden.' She should stop this now, explain the truth, but she couldn't, not when Jayne's spike heels were beating a hypnotic tattoo, inducing Aiden to follow her through the door.

The realtor walked over to a modest silver estate car that was parked across the street and unlocked the doors with the remote on her key fob. 'You know, I only just got this back from the auto shop. Can't hardly manage without it. The last person who was interested in the Millman place had to take me over there in her own SUV.'

With every word, more of the jigsaw began to fit together, but Aiden needed to hear the truth for herself. She said nothing as the car headed out on the highway, towards the beach house, wondering quite how to begin the conversation. In the end, she waited till they'd parked before the house, the tyre tracks of the blonde's SUV still visible in the hard-packed sand, and entered the house.

Curiosity filled her. She'd never been one for poking through strangers' houses, but something about this property called to her. Never having set foot in it while that self-absorbed ass of a film producer had been living here, she was keen to see what he'd done to the place. More than that, she wanted to spend as much time as she could in the company of this elegant, sexy woman in the mint-green dress that clung to the curves of her butt cheeks and breasts.

The kitchen was dominated by a huge range, and contained any number of labour-saving devices from a breadmaker to an espresso machine, none of which Aiden suspected had seen much use. She imagined herself making coffee and taking it through to the deck out front, with its uninterrupted view of the ocean. If she'd seriously been in the market for a new home, she'd already be putting in an offer; she could hardly understand why no one had already.

It was only when Jayne led her down the hallway to the master bedroom that Aiden spoke up. 'Before we go any further, I've got a confession to make.'

'Really?' Jayne arched an eyebrow.

'You know you were here last Friday with a client? Well – so was I. I didn't realise you were a realtor. I thought I knew everyone who works at Minola Beach Real Estate by sight, but obviously not. When I saw the two of you arrive, I thought you'd just bought the house, and I was keen to see who my new neighbours were. And – I kind of watched you.'

Jayne didn't say anything for a long moment, and

Aiden found herself wishing she could just sink though the floorboards. Then Jayne laughed; the sound bright and genuine. 'Oh, darling, that's so precious. Suzie's going to absolutely die when I tell her about this.'

'Please, don't, I'm so sorry.' Aiden began to back away, mortified.

'Don't worry. Suzie's an old friend of mine. The kind with benefits, if you know what I mean. She's looking for a property somewhere along the coast, so I showed her this place. It needs too much in the way of renovation for her, but – she enjoyed her viewing.' Jayne stepped closer. 'And it sounds like you enjoyed it too.'

'I –' Aiden couldn't get the words out. Jayne stilled them with a kiss. Her lips were soft and sweet, and when she increased the pressure, slipping her tongue into Aiden's mouth, there was no resisting. Aiden all but melted into Jayne's arms, allowing herself to be guided into the bedroom.

'You want this, don't you?' Jayne murmured.

Aiden gave a nod, all inhibitions blown away by this unexpected but so welcome seduction. Skilfully, Jayne set about stripping her of her T-shirt and low-slung jeans. They were dropped to the floor, along with her functional white bra. Jayne smiled as she regarded Aiden's bare breasts, capped with nipples that were already stiff.

'Let's get you comfortable, darling.' She helped Aiden on to the bed, before kicking off her shoes and joining her.

Now Aiden knew how Suzie had felt as she'd lain there, waiting for Jayne to love her with lips and tongue. Her pussy flowered against her underwear, lips plumping and glossing with her juices, and a pulse beat hard in her clit.

Jayne's tongue made slow, slippery progress over Aiden's collarbones, circling the peaks of her nipples before moving lower. 'Please,' Aiden heard herself murmur, 'lick me. Lick my pussy.'

'Are you sure, darling?'

Aiden had never been more sure of anything. She felt her breath catch as Jayne eased down her panties. The scent of her own arousal was sharp, overpowering, and she knew, as her underwear came off, that Jayne would see as well as smell just how excited she was.

She didn't have too much time to think what she might look like, sex lips slick and puffy, clit emerging from its sheltering hood, as Jayne plunged her mouth down. Aiden registered the feel of hot lips enclosing her clit, giving it a little sucking kiss. Pleasure sheared through her, making her grip handfuls of the comforter and jerk her hips up, wanting more of that hot, wet pressure on her most delicate place.

Jayne smiled at Aiden's almost frantic response, and pulled her lips away. 'Looks like it's been a while,' she observed. 'Well, slow down, it's not like we're going to be disturbed …'

With that, she rocked back on her haunches, reaching

behind herself to unzip the dress and let it slither down her body. Though Aiden had already studied Jayne's lingerie-clad curves, seeing them up close, rather than through a window, added a new dimension to her appreciation. The material was so sheer, every detail of Jayne's taut, tawny nipples and bush of flame-red hair was revealed through it.

Pushing Aiden back against the pillows, Jayne went to work once more. Now her tongue slithered over the insides of Aiden's thighs, circling her nether lips, dallying on the sensitive place between pussy and asshole, each fresh sensation melding with the next to lift Aiden closer to her peak. At Jayne's command, she rolled over, so her lover could lick her from behind, burying her nose in the dark cleft between Aiden's ass cheeks. No one had thought to pleasure her in this deliciously animalistic way before, and she buried her head in the pillows, mewling and humping her ass back at Jayne. The realtor's sinuous tongue slithered over Aiden's rear hole, rimming and promising to push its way inside. Two of Jayne's perfectly manicured fingers pushed up into Aiden's sex, fucking her with a steady in-and-out motion.

'God, yeah, that's it!' Aiden babbled, her words muffled by the pillow. It didn't matter that Jayne had been fucking another woman on this very same bed only a few days ago; for now, as her pleasure spiralled unstoppably up, there was no time but now, no other person in the world but the one licking her so expertly.

All sensations became one, and Aiden howled as her orgasm rolled through her, pounding her like storm-whipped waves against the beach outside.

Flopping down on the mattress, Aiden rolled on to her back and looked up into Jayne's smiling face. Her juices shone on the redhead's lips and chin, and she knew when they kissed she would be able to taste herself there.

'Nice?' Jayne asked.

All Aiden could do was nod, the power of speech temporarily stolen from her by the power of her orgasm.

'So, do you think you'll be putting in an offer?' As Jayne spoke, she flicked open the front catch of her bra, letting her tits fall free. 'Or would you like a little more time to explore all the amenities?'

'Don't you have to get back to the office?' Aiden asked, for the first time realising how much time they'd spent in the beach house. Jayne must have other, legitimate clients to deal with, after all.

'Nancy will cover for me. Now, where were we?' Jayne crawled up Aiden's body till her breast hung over Aiden's mouth, the nipple berry-ripe and almost begging to be sucked. Needing no further invitation, Aiden's lips closed round the firm bud and she began to suck.

'Oh, darling, where have you been till now?' Jayne sighed, pushing a hand down her panties to stroke her pussy, the movements of her fingers all too visible through the sheer fabric.

Suddenly, it didn't seem to matter to Aiden that the beach house might remain unsold a while longer. Not with this gorgeous realtor on hand to bring her up to the property and give her an intimate viewing whenever she might require one. She smiled, and reached up to pull Jayne's curvy body hard down on to her own.

Morning Glory
Giselle Renarde

Waking up next to Wanda was the greatest pleasure Janelle had ever experienced. And she experienced it at least four times before morning.

It was that goddamn waterbed. Wanda was heavier than Janelle, and every time she shifted, the water wave launched Janelle to the far side of the mattress. Same thing when Wanda got up in the middle of the night for a glass of water, or to pee afterwards. It was a night of interrupted sleep, but Janelle always awoke with a smile on her face because she was lying beside the woman she loved.

'What time is it?' Janelle asked when sunlight gleamed through the bedroom window.

'Hmm?' Wanda's sleepy fingers traipsed through Janelle's trimmed bush, playing with that curly hair.

Janelle held her breath. Everything felt so good. If she

97

breathed, it might fall away. So she held perfectly still while Wanda stroked the pink of her pussy lips. They were wet already, prepared for anything, and, when Wanda's fingertips met her sleepy clit, she gasped. Janelle was always at her most sensitive first thing in the morning.

'Time to get up and get showered.' Wanda's voice was thick with sleep. Her fingers retreated from Janelle's aroused flesh.

'Oh.' Janelle couldn't conceal her disappointment. It was Saturday. Neither of them had to work, and they had no firm plans for the day. Why couldn't Wanda crawl between Janelle's legs and lick her pussy?

Wanda rolled over and the ensuing waterbed wave sent Janelle flying. Bloody thing! It was like sleeping in a Moon Bounce.

Sunshine peeked through the slats of Wanda's white plastic blinds. The décor in this house was outdated, and that reminded Janelle that Wanda used to live here with a man – with a husband, a father of children. She felt a bit queasy if she lingered too long on that thought.

Janelle wandered into the bathroom and laughed when she realised she was standing naked in front of the open blinds. If Wanda's neighbours walked by, they'd get a good look at Janelle's bare breasts. She reached for the blinds, but Wanda grabbed her wrist. That deliberate force made Janelle weak in the knees, and she let herself ease back against Wanda's big boobs.

'Leave it open, little girl.' Wanda's voice was deep with lust, and it made Janelle feel small and susceptible.

'What if your neighbours see?'

Wanda shrugged behind her. Hands slid like snakes up Janelle's belly, toward her naked tits. 'So what? You shy about your body?'

'It's not that.' *Of course it was!* 'I just …'

The second Wanda's fingertips found her nipples, she was a goner. She couldn't think, couldn't speak, could hardly stand. All she could do was savour the pressure as Wanda rolled her nipples. God, she could feel it in her pussy, like her tits were connected directly to her clit.

Before realising it, Janelle had her fingers on her clit, rubbing there. Little bursts of electricity erupted as she stroked herself. She loved the way Wanda played with her tits. Not every woman got it right, but Wanda knew how much pressure Janelle wanted, how much pinching, how much squeezing.

Janelle struggled to keep her eyes open. It was exciting, standing in front of the open blinds and rubbing her pussy while her woman pinched her tits. She'd never been much of an exhibitionist, but she could sense a change within herself. Wanda was stretching her limits.

'Shower time!' Wanda pulled her in and turned on the water, one whirlwind motion. Janelle hugged her chest and screeched at the needling chill.

Wanda just laughed. She was tough – she could deal with anything, even a cold shower.

The water heated up fast, thank goodness, and warmth drove the chill from Janelle's skin. Wanda rubbed a bar of soap across Janelle's breasts, down her belly, settling against her bush. The shower water struck her front, washing the soapsuds away as fast as Wanda could create them.

Janelle swivelled to face her woman, and the cocky smirk on Wanda's lips turned her on more than she'd admit. 'I want to soap you up too.'

Their nipples and their bellies kissed as they hugged each other's hips. They were standing so close it was hard to tell where one body ended and the other began.

'We could do that,' Wanda teased. 'You wash my tits, I wash yours.'

'Yeah.' Janelle pressed her cheek to Wanda's chest. It was nice, dating a taller woman. She liked the idea of Wicked Wanda towering above her. 'Soapy pussies, soapy tits, soapy armpits, soapy ass cracks.' Janelle chuckled. 'We could spend all day finding new places to wash.'

'We *could* do that.' Wanda set her chin on top of Janelle's head, and it felt funny when she talked. 'But I've got a better idea.'

Wanda spun Janelle so the hot cascade struck her tits. Wet heat needled her nipples, making her gasp and then moan. 'Oh, God, babe, what are you gonna do to me?'

'Get down.' Wanda pressed her shoulders, but she resisted.

'What do you mean?'

'Down,' Wanda said, pushing her shoulders again. 'All the way down. Sit on the tub floor.'

Janelle followed instructions. To her surprise, when she went down Wanda went with her, cradling her head between those big breasts.

'Now walk your feet up on the wall.'

Janelle laughed, sputtering as the shower flow slapped her face. 'Walk my feet up how?'

Wanda knelt behind her, both hands supporting her sides. 'I want the soles of your feet flat on the tile, on either side of the faucet. I want your pussy right beneath it.'

Finally, it dawned on Janelle what Wanda was orchestrating: she was going to run the bathwater all over Janelle's gaping pussy.

'Well?' Wanda's voice was slick like oil. 'Whatcha waiting for, little girl?'

There was no good answer to that question, so Janelle didn't say anything. She just eased her body forward and walked her feet up the wall until her heels rested on either side of the faucet. Her head slumped into Wanda's lap so all she saw when she looked up were Wanda's big tits. God, she wanted to nibble those nipples but, just as she craned her head, Wanda switched the cascade from shower to tub.

Water rushed from the faucet in one violent stream, striking Janelle's pussy and sending splashes across her legs and up her belly. Wanda urged Janelle to raise her ass off the tub floor and tilt her pelvis until the cascade struck her clit. It seemed impossible, but the reward of warm water pounding her sensitive clit seemed worth the inelegance of the journey. Pressing her head into Wanda's lap, she inched her feet up the tile, tilting her hips until the cascade struck her clit. Hard.

With a shriek of tortured pleasure, Janelle closed her thighs to the flow. Bathwater splashed the tile and the stream struck her square in the ass, but that was bearable. Actually, it felt damn good.

Wanda slid her hands between Janelle's thighs. 'Open your legs!'

The moment that torrent landed against her clit, Janelle screamed, 'No!'

'Why not?' Wanda's hands were still wedged between Janelle's legs.

'It's too much.' Janelle fought to close her thighs, all the while resigning herself to lose. Wanda was stronger. Anyway, Janelle didn't want to win this battle. 'It feels too good!'

'If it feels so good, why don't you want it? Can't handle your orgasms, little girl?'

'I always could before I met you.' Janelle laughed, but it was true. Wanda was an incredible lover, forceful and aggressive, but always tender enough to stay on her good side.

The water pounded Janelle when Wanda rocked her. 'We'll take it slow. We'll work our way there.'

'Where?'

'Here!' Wanda surprised Janelle by splitting her legs open, exposing her tender clit to the flow.

How could a liquid be so hard? Janelle screamed, pushed back, lodged her head against Wanda's naked belly. It was like mud wrestling, but cleaner.

Wanda was strong, but merciful. With one hand she blocked the flow, and Janelle relaxed. 'I thought you said I could work my way up to that!'

'Yeah.' Wanda chuckled. 'But you're cute when you scream.'

Janelle's throat was raw after shrieking and her clit felt huge, like a red pulsing monster between her legs. 'Right.'

Without asking what to do, Janelle tilted her pelvis so the water plunged deep inside her pussy. The cascade assaulted her, filling that hollow with warm water until her pussy overflowed. Sprays shot from between her legs, splashing her thighs and the tile while streams ran down her ass crack.

It didn't hurt, not like it had when the flow banged her clit. Even that didn't *hurt*, but it was too much pleasure. This was different. Janelle thrust toward the faucet. The flow was even harsher there, harder, more concentrated, and the water splashed against the tile wall as she fucked the bath. This felt amazing, but there was something more she wanted. Janelle had an itch only the cascade could scratch, and it throbbed at the surface of her engorged clit.

Wanda seemed to know what Janelle was thinking, because painstakingly slowly, she opened her fingers, allowing just a bit of water between them. As soon as Janelle felt a little bit, she wanted a lot. Wanda tortured her. Janelle traced her hips in circles, trying to get away from Wanda's fingers, or at least line them up so more water would flow between them.

And then Wanda rubbed Janelle's clit, and her orgasm was instantaneous. She didn't see it coming, and suddenly it was on her, all over her, making her writhe against Wanda's thighs. Those fingers knew what to do, stroking just where she needed them, deep motion, hard motion, just like the water.

'Had enough?' Wanda asked while Janelle flopped about the tub floor like a fish.

How could she possibly answer? Her pussy was palpitating, spurting water like fireworks. She'd come so hard she couldn't keep still, but she was greedy. If there was more pleasure coming to her, she wanted it all.

When she didn't answer, Wanda said, 'I think you're after another orgasm.'

With a breathy chuckle, Janelle admitted, 'I'm always after another orgasm.'

'Good,' Wanda said. 'Then I'll give you one.'

Positioning Janelle's orgasmic pussy under the tap, Wanda stole her fingers away. The cascade bombarded Janelle's clit with all its wet hot force. She gasped and tried to pull away, but Wanda grabbed her hips and held her in place. Though the spray from the bath misted her face, Janelle watched that clear flow pound her clit, parting her pussy lips before rebounding in all directions.

Wanda opened Janelle's pussy lips so the bathwater smacked her clit unhindered. Janelle thrust toward the faucet, wanting more – more heat, more hard, more pleasure. She'd never felt anything so intense, ever, in her entire sexual life. As Wanda held her pussy lips apart, Janelle grabbed her own nipples and squeezed.

That was it. Janelle was a goner. The pleasure shot like a lightning bolt straight to her clit, and it was explosive. That one little squeeze pushed the balance from just enough to far too much. She screamed, pressing her feet so hard against the tile that she managed to do some version of a backflip away from the faucet. God only knows how she ended up kneeling behind Wanda, but it made them both laugh.

Wanda shut off the faucet and stood to open the shower curtain. Janelle shivered. Her pussy was a hot, wet, pulsing hunger, despite her intense satisfaction.

'Come on, get up.' Wanda grabbed her hands and

helped her out of the tub. 'I'll make you a big breakfast after that little workout.'

Janelle stood naked and dripping in front of the open blinds. Through the window she watched an older woman walk six bichons frisés on multicoloured leashes. It was such an odd sight, those six little dogs yapping at the lady's feet, that Janelle couldn't draw away.

When the old woman looked up at the bathroom window, eyes widening at the sight of Janelle's naked body, Wanda laughed. 'Putting on a show for my neighbours, eh?'

Janelle smirked. 'I'm too worn out to care.'

Wanda smacked Janelle's ass so hard it stung. 'Dry off,' she said, handing Janelle a towel. 'Time to eat.'

Janelle's hair was still wet when she sat at Wanda's breakfast table wearing nothing but a cheery yellow towel. Over at the counter, Wanda was completely naked.

'Want help with anything?' Janelle asked, standing and slowly approaching her girlfriend.

'I've got it under control,' Wanda replied without so much as a glance in Janelle's direction. She seemed to be doing a hundred things at once, flitting from waffle iron to refrigerator to sink.

'You sure?' Janelle snuck behind the counter and smoothed her palms over Wanda's sweet round ass. Growling, she squeezed, sinking her fingernails into her woman's gorgeous flesh.

Wanda jumped, yelping, 'Little bitch!'

'Oh, am I?' Janelle giggled. She didn't let go.

With a hissed breath, Wanda turned to meet Janelle's gaze. Her dark eyes danced with a new brand of lust, hooking into Janelle's desire, capturing her completely. And then she said, 'Sit at the table or I'll to strap you to that chair.'

The waffle iron's light flicked on, indicating breakfast was ready, and Janelle gave in to her hunger. She and Wanda had gone at each other so many times since dinner last night that her stomach was eating itself.

With a deliberate sigh, Janelle released Wanda's ass cheeks. A tremor of joy rippled through her core when she spotted the little red nail marks she'd left in her wake. She chuckled to herself as she sauntered into the sunlight shining through the sliding glass doors. The backyard garden was surprisingly lovely, raised beds all blooming with pink and purple flowers.

'Your backyard is beautiful.' Janelle tilted her head and smiled. 'I can't picture you as a gardener.'

Wanda laughed as she poured more batter into the hot iron. 'Trust me, I'm not. Flowers pop up every spring and the kids take care of the weeding. Henry was the expert. He built all those boxes, not to mention the deck out there.'

Janelle's throat ran dry. This happened every time she heard the name 'Henry'. She wished she could be more mature, but it hurt. Just the idea of him hurt.

As Wanda waltzed naked through the kitchen, transporting little bowls of berries, butter, whipped cream and other foodstuffs from counter to table, Janelle tried to imagine the woman married to a man. No, she couldn't do it. The whole idea felt weird and unsettling, like it took something away from their relationship. When Wanda mentioned family matters, Janelle didn't know how to respond.

'Do the kids spend a lot of weekends with your parents?' Janelle asked, staring at the washed berries. They sparkled with little beads of water. 'I mean, now that Henry's ...'

Why was it so hard to talk about this stuff?

Wanda didn't answer right away. She brought a heaping plate of waffles to the table and plunked herself in the chair next to Janelle's. 'I think Gran and Poppa will be watching the kids more often, now that you're in my life. Nice to have a little private time in an empty house, just us adults.'

Janelle couldn't argue there, and she certainly didn't argue when Wanda slid a hand up her thigh. In fact, Janelle encouraged the action even as she shovelled dry waffles into her mouth. 'Mmm ... that feels good.'

'I bet it does.' Wanda inched her chair closer, finding Janelle's pubic hair with her fingertips. 'Hey, why'd I whip up all these fixings if you're gonna eat your waffles plain?'

'Sorry,' Janelle said, talking with her mouth full. 'I'm just so hungry. I couldn't wait.'

'You couldn't wait, huh?' Wanda's fingers sank down past her tender clit and pressed inside her pussy. 'What else can't you wait for?'

Janelle moaned, 'More.'

The pad of Wanda's thumb landed on Janelle's clit, rubbing in tight circles. 'Yeah, you like that.'

The languorous pace of Wanda's stroking made Janelle writhe in her chair. It felt good, of course it did, but her poor sizzling flesh needed a little break.

'Babe, I'm too sore right now.' Closing her thighs around Wanda's hand, Janelle pushed her chair back and finished chewing her waffle. She stood, unfolding her towel and opening it like a pair of wings.

Wanda leaned back in her chair, looking Janelle up and down, her expression positively wolfish. 'Too sore, huh?'

Nodding coyly, Janelle approached her woman. She tried to look aloof and alluring as a runway model when she dropped her towel to the floor. 'Why don't you let me take care of you for once, babe?' Janelle picked up a strawberry and traced it between Wanda's big breasts, then leaned forward to follow its trail with her tongue.

Wanda hissed, but said, 'Sit and eat your breakfast.'

All innocent-like, Janelle picked up the bowl of whipped cream and used her strawberry to slather fluffy whiteness across Wanda's dark nipples. 'You hardly ever let me do nice things to you.'

Without waiting for a response, Janelle nuzzled Wanda's nipple, getting a dollop of whipped cream stuck to her nose. Playing cute and coquettish, she raised her face to Wanda's and her woman kissed the cream away. Janelle fed the tip of her big strawberry to Wanda and then ate the fat base herself. It was juicy and sweet – perfect fruit.

'Let me lick your tits?' Janelle pleaded. They looked so hot with white peaks like meringues covering both nipples.

Wanda smiled warmly. 'I guess you'd better; now you got me all sticky.'

Janelle didn't waste a moment. She tossed her strawberry stem on to Wanda's plate, pressed those big tits together and devoured whipped cream. The sweetness danced on her palate as she sucked one pebbled nipple. Janelle's cheeks were already sticky when she moved to the other tit, swallowing and wanting more.

'God, I love your boobs.' Janelle rubbed her face against that soft, yielding flesh. She kissed both breasts, squeezed them, licked, sucked, while Wanda reached for the berry bowl.

'What else do you love?' Wanda raised her pelvis enough for Janelle to get a look at that dark, glistening pussy.

Janelle plucked a colossal strawberry from the bowl and traced the tip down Wanda's rounded stomach. 'I love your belly.'

Wanda cooed as the berry left a wet trail to the dark border of her pubic hair. 'Is that all you love?'

'No way.' Janelle set the fat side of that huge berry against Wanda's clit and rubbed gently.

Wanda gasped and gazed down, though she probably couldn't see past those mammoth tits. Even without the dollops of whipped cream, Wanda's nipples were alluring beyond belief. How could Janelle resist? She leaned in close to suck each tit in turn, all the while stroking her woman's clit with the strawberry.

'Oh, God.' Wanda rolled her hips slowly, beckoningly. 'I can feel all the little seeds against me.'

Janelle didn't even release Wanda's nipple to ask, 'Is that bad?'

'No, no, no,' Wanda replied in quick little pants. 'No, it's goooood!'

When Wanda's body began to shudder, belly rippling and boobs bouncing, Janelle rubbed harder with that big fat berry. Only Wanda's toes touched the floor now, while her thighs trembled and her arms wrapped tightly around Janelle's back. Janelle switched breasts, sucking one nipple, sucking the other, everything full-out because Wanda was so close to the brink.

The fruit's flesh seemed firm enough to stand up to just

about anything, and Janelle was determined to put it to the test. She rubbed so hard her fingers poked through the flesh. The berry wasn't indestructible after all, but Janelle didn't stop stroking. Wanda had one hand in her hair now, gripping it in a tight fist and wailing under a dense climax. Still, Janelle rubbed hard, until the strawberry turned to mush against Wanda's clit.

Janelle shifted back and chuckled at the sight of red fruit flesh smooshed into Wanda's pubic hair. 'You came fast, babe.'

'You made me.' Wanda's breasts heaved as she struggled for breath.

Janelle grabbed the whole bowl of berries and sank to her knees. Sunlight streamed through the sliding glass doors, warming her naked backside as she leaned between her woman's open legs. 'I've got a few more tricks up my sleeve.'

'What kinds of tricks?'

There was another huge strawberry in the bowl, this one even bigger than the last. Wanda gasped when the strawberry's white little tip met the gleaming lips of her pussy. 'What are you doing?'

'Shoving a strawberry up your snatch,' Janelle said simply, like this was something she did every day.

When Janelle eased the berry slowly into that gorgeous wet slit, Wanda shivered. 'Oooh, that's cold.'

It was no easy task, fucking a woman with a strawberry

without tearing off the leafy green stem, but Janelle worked with focused diligence. She loved the way Wanda's pussy opened up to accommodate the fruit's bulging shape. She wanted to give Wanda every pleasure in the world, and the big blueberries lining the berry bowl inspired another idea. Janelle pulled the giant strawberry out of Wanda's snatch and fed it to her, pressing a blueberry inside before those keen pussy muscles could tighten up again.

Furrowing her brow, Wanda glanced down and asked, 'What'd you do, little girl?'

Janelle planted a wet kiss against Wanda's engorged clit. 'I just shoved a blueberry in your pussy.'

Wanda tossed her head back and laughed. 'How do you plan on getting it back out?'

'Like this.' Janelle danced her tongue down Wanda's slit, then set her lips around that juicy hole and inhaled. The suction worked like a charm, and that fat little berry soared into her mouth. She chewed it with a cocky smile, savouring the tartness of the blueberry with the accompanying tanginess of Wanda's pussy.

'Well, aren't you a clever little minx?' Wanda's smile said she wanted more.

Scooping up a handful of blueberries, Janelle pressed the little spheres into the heat of Wanda's pussy. Each time, she poked her finger inside a little farther and kept it in a little longer, making Wanda moan.

'You'll be full of blueberries.' Janelle poked another one in, then tickled Wanda's clit with her tongue. She forced another blueberry inside, and another finger, exploring Wanda's wet heat. That juicy flesh was soft beyond soft, and the more she licked, the harder that surprisingly tight sex hugged her fingers. Three now. She really wanted Wanda to feel her presence.

Wanda tossed her head to one side and moaned, 'Fuck, you're gonna crush them. I'm gonna be full of blueberry jam.'

Janelle chuckled even as she licked Wanda's clit, which was already covered in crushed strawberry. Yes, the blueberries were getting mushy in there, but her fingers loved Wanda's pussy and they didn't want to leave just yet.

'Think I can make you come again?' Janelle teased. The answer was obvious – Wanda was nearing the edge already.

Wanda didn't answer, except to offer high-pitched squeals while Janelle sucked her fat clit. Wanda's pussy tasted good, so damn sweet from the fruit. Her body began to vibrate, and her pussy muscles squeezed Janelle's fingers like crazy.

'Suck it!' Wanda howled, bucking against Janelle's mouth. 'Suck those berries out!'

Janelle did as she was told, pinching Wanda's clit between her finger and thumb as she stole her other hand away from that packed pussy. Wrapping her lips around Wanda's slit to form a tight seal, she started sucking. The mushed berries didn't leap into her mouth quite as fast as the whole ones, but once Janelle build up enough suction, her mouth filled with tangy-sweet jam. Blueberry-pussy jam, a delicacy.

She pinched Wanda's clit, letting it slip and slide between her fingers, and that did the trick. Wanda pitched her pussy against Janelle's mouth. The motion was frenzied, and Janelle struggled to stay latched to Wanda's pussy. When Wanda jerked her thighs together, Janelle backed off and watched her twitch and writhe naked in her chair, as though some phantom being were still pleasuring her.

Swallowing the last bit of that blueberry-pussy mixture, Janelle found her towel on the kitchen floor and sprawled like a pin-up model. 'That was a first.'

'For me, too.' Wanda's big tits heaved with each breath.

'You mean your husband never sucked blueberries from your snatch?' Janelle asked, immediately mortified by her own words.

But Wanda didn't seem fazed. 'No, Henry was always more interested in putting something else inside me.'

Janelle's stomach lurched at the image. 'Sorry. I shouldn't have said that.'

'Henry died almost ten years ago.' Wanda's expression turned downy. 'If I couldn't talk about the man, I'd know I wasn't ready to be in a new relationship yet – with you, or with anyone.'

'OK.' Janelle wasn't sure how to feel about that. Maybe she was being immature, but it was easier to pretend Wanda had never been married at all.

'Hey, little girl.' Wanda patted her lap, and Janelle rested her head there. Wanda smelled musky and berry-sweet, which made her smile. 'It's like everything in life – gets easier with time. I know it's strange for you, being here, but one day you won't think of this house as *mine*. You'll think of it as *ours*. Right?'

Nodding against Wanda's soft thigh, Janelle thought how silly it was that the woman who'd lost her husband was sitting there consoling the woman who'd never even lost a set of keys. Wanda was right – Janelle was a little girl, still uninitiated into the adult worlds of family and commitment. But that was changing now. Janelle could feel the change inside her belly, sprouting like a seed. In Wanda's house, and in Wanda's life, that seed would take root. *Hers* would one day become *theirs*.

Janelle kissed Wanda's thigh, making her twitch. 'I love you, babe.'

They breathed together, eyes closed, chests rising and falling languidly.

Running a hand across Janelle's sun-warmed shoulder, Wanda said, 'I love you too.'

Under the Slippers
Annabeth Leong

Eva leaned back against Katya, her expensive French scent mingling with the smell of leather rising from the white couch where they planned to spend the evening. The antique clock in the corner ticked, the only sound in the room besides their breathing. Katya's long, skilled fingers traced the lines of Eva's sleeves, found her hands and rubbed at the fleshy parts of her palms.

'You have knots in the muscles of your hands,' Katya murmured, her slight Russian accent lending its aura of worldliness to even her simplest sentences. 'I thought your nail girl would have massaged those out of you.'

Eva shrugged and closed her eyes. She didn't want to talk about Tara from the day spa, but the nail tech had become Katya's favourite subject in the last few weeks. She started to mumble a vague reply, but Katya gasped and dropped Eva's hands as if they had bitten her.

Eva snapped to attention. 'Katya? What's the matter?'

'Your nails! Have you been biting them?'

'People bite their nails, Katya. It's not an emergency.'

'Not you. You don't bite your nails.' Katya tugged Eva around to face her and shook her head, her ice-blue eyes fervent and wide in the pale canvas of her carefully made-up face. 'Let me see your toes. Now.'

Eva cringed and lifted her feet onto the couch beside them, braced this time for Katya's theatrical shriek.

'You have tip wear! And they're the same colour they were last week!'

'Did you give up finance to become the fashion police?'

Katya clicked her tongue and nudged Eva out of her lap. 'I wouldn't care if it was someone else. But I know you, Eva.'

Eva twisted her slim brown foot and studied it from different angles. The sapphire finish on her perfectly shaped toenails would have alarmed no one but Katya – even after several weeks, it still looked polished and fashionable. She flicked the gold charm bracelet she wore around her ankle and curled her toes so the rings on them glinted. She still had pretty feet, cared for far better than most.

The tip of Katya's fingernail ran over a callus beginning below Eva's big toe. Eva suppressed her inner shiver at even that slight contact to her foot. Katya raised her elegantly plucked blonde eyebrow and tapped the callus significantly.

'You're right.' Eva sighed. 'I haven't skipped a weekly pedicure since sophomore year of college.'

Katya pressed a light kiss to the back of Eva's neck. 'Is it work?'

Eva shook her head.

Katya's grip on Eva shifted, her long nails digging into Eva's green suit jacket and pinching the skin underneath. 'Are you avoiding nail girl?'

'Her name's Tara.'

'You're never going to ask her out, are you?'

'Not if you keep bothering me about it.'

'You're bothering yourself. Skipping your pedicure just to put off having to gather a little courage!'

Eva exhaled and turned toward Katya. The Russian blonde's long legs folded into an unnatural yet graceful position that revealed her years of ballet training at the hands of strict Soviet masters. A frown wrinkled the otherwise unlined skin of her tanned forehead. Eva rubbed a finger over Katya's knuckles. 'I don't understand why you care so much about me getting a date with this girl.' She turned her caress into a light scratch, watching for the sensual awakening that dawned in Katya's eyes. 'Is it so terrible to have me around here on Friday nights?'

Katya slid a few inches away from Eva. 'You deserve better than this. You should have a real girlfriend.'

Eva recognised one of Katya's cynical moods coming on. She flung herself into the other woman's lap, knowing her thin, slight body would present no discomfort. 'And that can't be you?'

Katya looked away for a moment, then sighed and returned to Eva with a voracious kiss. Her teeth nibbled Eva's lower lip until Eva whimpered and squirmed in Katya's grasp. Katya released her with a heavy breath.

'Eva, you know how much I care about you. But we're not enough for each other.' Katya stroked the sole of Eva's foot, inspiring a hissing, indrawn breath and a clench between Eva's legs. 'You need to be with someone who lets you play with her feet.' Katya lifted one elegant leg, showing her slipper-covered foot, the object of Eva's most intense imaginings. No amount of longing, salivating or begging had ever earned Eva the right to worship that foot. Katya hated her feet to be touched or even seen – something about the damage inflicted by all those ballet lessons.

The Russian woman cleared her throat, redirecting Eva's attention from the embroidered red satin fitted over that mysterious foot. 'For me, on the other hand, I want a woman who likes pain. More than a nibble here or there.'

Eva hung her head, unable to argue with the iron-clad logic of their incompatible fetishes. But the logic of her heart worked differently – she could imagine no sexual arrangement that did not include Katya, no matter how alluring Tara could be. She tongued the spot behind

Katya's ear, speaking her mind through the language of sex rather than with words.

The doorbell rang, and Eva jerked upright. She glanced at the red numerals of Katya's antique clock. 'It's late. Who could that be?'

Katya's lips curled into a secret, private shape. 'A surprise visitor,' she said. 'More of a surprise, I suppose, because of that pedicure you skipped.' Katya untangled her legs and floated to open the door.

Eva adjusted her dishevelled business attire. 'Katya, what are you talking about?'

The Russian woman opened her heavy dark-wood door and stood aside to reveal Tara the nail girl in all her plump, rosy loveliness. She wore the same pastel apron she did at work and carried a large flowered bag over one shoulder. She gifted Katya with a shy smile, then shared it with Eva.

Eva stared from one to the other, noting the triumph on Katya's face and the way Tara chewed at the corner of one pale-pink lip. 'What's going on, Katya?'

'I asked Tara to come do pedicures for us,' Katya said, as if it were the most natural thing in the world.

The shock of Tara's appearance faded before the momentous implications of Katya's pronoun. 'Us?' Eva stared at the ever-present slippers.

'How many times have you told me she gives the best pedicures ever?'

'But that was –' Eva cut herself off, afraid to explain herself in front of Tara. She could not say anything here and now about the delicious patience with which Tara rubbed brown sugar-scented lotion into her feet, nor of how far up the leg her fingers travelled, nor of the spectacular view of the dark-haired beauty's generous cleavage, squeezed together and quivering as she worked to give Eva pleasure.

Katya grinned and winked, surely reading the thoughts on Eva's face. She gestured Tara in, apologising for keeping her waiting at the door.

Tara paused just inside, blinking. Eva could not blame her. Katya's living room, white as sacramental linen but for a few crimson accents, had a sort of religious splendour. Tara set down her flowered bag on a snow-coloured carpet thick enough to swallow it. She cleared her throat. 'I'll need hot water.'

'Down the hall and to the right,' Katya said. She returned to the couch with her cool demeanour intact, but her hand trembled when she touched Eva's.

Eva watched Tara's generous round ass recede, then leaned to whisper in Katya's ear. 'Really, what the hell is going on?'

'Don't you like your surprise?'

'I can't believe you want *her* to give *you* a pedicure.'

Katya's icy eyes narrowed and cut toward Eva. 'Why? Are you jealous?'

Eva considered the question. She was jealous, but the feeling was eclipsed by her eagerness to see Katya's feet and to feel Tara's soft, strong fingers between her toes. 'I think I'll forgive you.'

Katya squeezed Eva's hand. 'Maybe this will work out for all of us.' She took a deep breath. 'All I know is, if I'm going to let someone touch my feet, I need privacy and I need you with me.'

'I'm here,' Eva said. She did not dare ask if she too could touch Katya's feet. She feared upsetting the delicate balance of the impending miracle.

'Good.' Anxiety and anticipation heated Katya's kiss. Her tongue thrust and curled as she helped Eva out of her suit jacket and toyed with her breasts through her cream silk blouse. Eva surrendered to the familiar touch, caught up in thoughts of Katya's toes.

Tara reminded the other two women of her presence by clearing her throat as she returned to the room. Eva jerked away from Katya, her face hot and red. 'I'm sorry,' she began.

The sugar scent Eva loved rolled from the sloshing basin Tara set on the carpet. Tara smiled hesitantly. 'Katya asked if I would mind. I said I wouldn't.' Her chest heaved as she glanced at the Russian woman. 'Actually, she made it sound like I'd be walking into a dimly lit, dildo-scattered room, with the two of you naked and fingering each other on the couch.'

Eva blinked. Tara's voice was sweet as her face – it would have been hard to imagine her saying 'dildo' in such a casual tone if it hadn't just happened.

Tara's smile widened in response to Eva's stunned expression. She dropped to her knees, picked up Eva's right foot, slipped off the toe rings and set them in a small holder attached to the basin. Her gentle touch sent lightning up Eva's leg and straight to her sex. Eva bit the inside of her cheek to keep from moaning aloud.

Tara's fingers crept up Eva's foot toward the ankle. The pad of her thumb rubbed a slow circle over the knob of bone before she unclasped the charm bracelet. The tiny worked gold shapes attached to the chain played havoc with Eva's pricking nerves as Tara tugged the jewellery away from Eva's foot and deposited it too in the holder. Eva squirmed and fisted her hands at her sides.

The soft, maddening touches continued. Tara stripped Eva's left foot bare as well and caressed it, finding calluses and sensitive spots. She slid both feet into a heavenly bath of warm, scented water. The textured surface of the bottom of the basin sent aching pleasure into the soles of Eva's feet every time she rubbed against it.

Katya's arms slid around Eva, and those touches mingled with the intense, shooting sensation coming from Eva's feet. Eva moaned.

'You are making her so wet right now,' Katya said, pulling Eva's skirt up to reveal a damp spot on her panties. The scent of arousal flooded the room, transforming Katya's cold, imposing living room into a primal, animal place.

Eva, her reactions slowed by pleasure, coloured and reached for her skirt. She met Tara's eyes. 'I'm sorry. I don't want to make you uncomfortable.'

Tara smiled gently. 'I'm not. I can usually smell you.' She looked up at Katya through her eyelashes and lifted another rubberised basin. 'I need to get water for this one, too.'

When she disappeared down the hall, Katya burst out laughing. 'I knew this woman had your number. The things you described – no way could she have acted that way without knowing you were getting off on it.' Katya's thumb tweaked Eva's chin. 'You are as red as my throw pillows.'

Eva's face burned ever more hotly. 'I didn't want to creep her out.'

'I think it's safe to say she's not creeped out. She's having fun.'

Tara returned bearing another basin of water. She knelt before Katya with striking reverence, gazing at the statuesque Russian with big, wide eyes. 'May I remove your slippers?'

Katya grabbed at Eva's hand and squeezed hard enough to grind the bones together. Her eyes were hooded, glinting coldly. 'You may.'

Eva glanced from Katya to Tara, trying to interpret the strict formality of their interaction. But speculation yielded to excitement. Eva held her breath as Tara lifted Katya's left foot and unbuttoned the strap of the red slipper that covered it. Katya's entire body went stiff. Tara paused.

Eva frowned. 'Are you OK?'

Katya nodded. 'Keep going,' she ordered Tara. A deep blush showed around her collar and spread up her neck.

'Are you turned on?' Eva whispered.

Katya responded with a strangled cry. Tara, never taking her eyes off the blonde woman's face, peeled the red satin slipper away from her long foot. Katya mewled in the back of her throat.

The foot Tara revealed was callused and cracked, the toes twisted, the nails black. Eva watched entranced as Tara stroked it and Katya shook from the effort of enduring the pleasure of her touch.

The elegant Russian's lips thinned with shame. 'That is not the beautiful thing you have dreamed about, I am sure.'

Tears welled in Eva's eyes. 'I would kiss it if you would let me.'

Shock flashed across Katya's face before she buried it behind her customary arch expression. 'Put it in the water, Tara, and then unwrap the other one.' Tara seemed to take no notice of the clipped, harsh tone of Katya's voice.

Katya's breath hissed out through her teeth as Tara

eased her feet into the basin. She closed her eyes a moment, and no one in the room could breathe. When she opened them again, her vulnerability had passed.

'Back to Eva for now, please,' she said.

Tara obeyed with an excited alacrity that puzzled Eva. She would have asked about it, but Tara's touch returning to the slippery skin of her feet rendered her speechless. Eva could not contain her moans as Tara rubbed handfuls of sugar scrub against the sides and soles of her feet, grinding it in with the heels of her hands and working the agonising pleasure deep into Eva's muscles.

Katya undid the buttons of Eva's blouse, then lifted her breasts from her bra cups. Eva gave herself over to two sets of irresistible hands.

'Tara,' Katya said, 'I know Eva is still worrying about you, somewhere in the back of her mind. Why don't you tell her how you feel so she can cut it out and have an orgasm?'

Katya's warm mouth closed around Eva's nipple, tonguing it hard before delivering a quick, sharp bite that made Eva yelp. Tara worked the scrub up her feet, to her calves, and all the way up to her knee. Katya tugged Eva's skirt up again and Tara's hands travelled even higher, the sweet-smelling grit abrasive against Eva's trembling inner thighs.

'Don't forget to talk, Tara,' Katya said, and applied her ministrations to Eva's other breast in turn.

Tara's hands froze and slipped a little way down to a safer spot on Eva's legs. Katya pulled them back into their previous position. She spoke once more, an undertone of feline threat lacing her voice. 'I hope I don't have to interrupt myself again.'

'I'm sorry,' Tara said. Lust thickened her stammer. 'Um, I think Eva has beautiful feet. Beautiful everything, really. I've had a crush on her for ages, ever since I figured out how much she likes what I do to her feet.'

Katya guided Tara's hands to Eva's panties. She briefly released Eva's nipple to suggest Tara tug them off. Tara's soft, scented fingers fumbled at the elastic of Eva's panties as Katya devoured one breast then the other. Katya stirred, but Tara resumed speaking before she could be admonished again.

'I've, um, never done anything like this, though. Never kissed a girl. I'd never have done anything about my feelings for Eva if you hadn't come to talk to me, Katya.'

'But you've masturbated thinking about Eva, of course.' Katya trailed nipping kisses down Eva's stomach, both tickling and inflicting sharp flashes of pain. Eva lifted her head to see Tara's response to this – the nail tech's pale, plump lips opened in the most delectable sort of shock, and her sweet, pointed tongue darted past her even, white teeth as if for a taste of the thought. Katya smirked and let the question pass.

'How often do you get off on women at the spa?' Katya

dipped her head lower, beginning to nose at Eva's slit. In a lower voice, she added, 'I think you've taken on more than you can handle this far up her leg. Get back to work on her feet. You'll have no trouble driving her crazy that way.'

Tara kissed Eva's knee and retreated from her thighs. She sluiced the scrub away with warm water made thick and silken by coconut oil. She scraped a pumice stone lightly over the calluses beginning to form on Eva's feet, its rough touch complementing the swipes of Katya's tongue over Eva's clit. The power of Eva's foot fetish made Tara's stone as much of a sensual torment as Katya's licks. Eva writhed in their grasp, spread her toes, and lifted her ass to give them both better access.

'Eva's the only client who gets my attention,' Tara said. 'I like the way she responds to me.' She hesitated until Katya lifted her head slightly from its position between Eva's legs, then went on speaking in a rush. 'But we also get free services, from the other girls at the spa, you know.'

'Which one gets you wet, Tara?' Katya's purring breath warmed Eva's sex.

'Jennifer, the one who does the waxing,' Tara confessed.

'When she waxes your pussy?'

'When she waxes anything.' Tara's hands shook around Eva's feet. She removed the pumice stone and returned with cool, maple-scented lotion. 'The way she rips the wax away hurts, but –'

129

'But you like it.'

'Yes.'

Eva felt Katya's smile. One of her long, elegant fingers pierced through Eva's folds and into her. Katya increased the pace of her tongue to match the stabbing rhythm of her finger-fucking. The contrast with Tara's sweet, caressing touch made each sensation all the sharper. Katya's thumb replaced her tongue, grinding Eva's clit in a circle so intense it would have hurt terribly had it not called forth a powerful orgasm.

Eva cried out, feeling the rippling ache of it between her toes and everywhere Tara touched, in addition to the clench between her legs.

Katya grinned down at Eva, but continued her patient questioning of Tara. Her fingers never ceased to manipulate Eva. 'Is that why you've waxed every part of your body? Arms included?'

'Yes,' Tara answered breathlessly.

'Suck Eva's toes,' Katya said.

Eva made a sound of protest, uncertain whether she could survive more pleasure. Tara's tongue flicked against the web between Eva's big and smaller toes. Not even the feeling of Katya's tongue on Eva's clit had gone to her head so rapidly. Eva squirmed, barely able to keep from jerking her foot away from the excruciating joy of Tara's mouth.

'That's it,' Katya said. 'Show me how you would lick her if I put your face in her pussy.'

Another tentative, electric lick, then Tara forgot her hesitation and laved Eva's foot with unashamed abandon. Eva's hands grasped at the air as she flailed. Katya's finger hooked inside Eva and pressed against her inner wall, inflicting sharp pleasure that forced Eva upright as a desperate orgasm took hold of her.

Katya sealed the moment with a sticky, sex-scented kiss to Eva's lips. Then she reached down and caught a length of Tara's hair. 'You can stop that now. You've done well.'

Tara released Eva's foot, panting. She blinked and swayed, obviously dazed by the sudden halt Katya had called.

Katya jerked on the hair. 'Look at me, Tara. You just look to me. I'll give you all the guidance you need.'

Tara's eyes opened wider. She rose suddenly and caught Katya in a passionate kiss. Katya's feet splashing in her basin betrayed her surprise, then her passion. Her fingers curled around the back of Tara's neck.

When Tara pulled back from Katya, she darted a guilty glance at Eva. 'Please don't take that the wrong way.' She bit her lip, shifting from foot to foot. Tara seemed unable to decide which woman commanded her eye contact.

Eva well understood the extent of Katya's magnetism. She smiled reassuringly at Tara and towelled her feet quickly so she could climb out of the basin. Stepping to Tara's side, she gathered the other woman's clothed body against her near-naked one, the stiff fabric of Tara's apron rough against her nipples. With gentle insistence, she pulled Tara into a soft kiss, tasting both herself and Katya on the pale, silky lips. 'You needed someone to give you permission to follow your desires, didn't you?' Eva murmured, pitching her voice low enough that only Tara could hear. 'Katya didn't just indulge you, she compelled you to give in.'

Tara bit her lower lip and nodded.

'Maybe you started out wanting me, but by now you can't escape your thoughts of her.'

'I do like you —'

Eva silenced her with another kiss, remembering her own pleas to Katya not long before. She pinched the flesh beside Tara's spine, savouring the responding tremor through the curvy woman's body, and the way she moaned and snuggled closer. Eva squeezed harder, twisting until she knew it hurt, but Tara's kiss only heated in response to the pain.

Releasing her, Eva brushed a lock of hair away from her eyes. Katya watched them from the couch, her face a mystery. Eva's heart pounded as knowledge and desire rose within her. 'Shall we serve her together?' she asked Tara.

With another submissive glance in Katya's direction, Tara nodded. As one, she and Eva fell to their knees in the thick white carpet.

Katya stared at them on the floor beside each other. 'What just happened?'

Eva leaned up and caught her old friend and lover's lips against hers, again using sex to speak the thoughts that came so reluctantly to her lips. She felt the tension in Katya's body, the anxiety that lurked just beneath her smooth veneer. Eva kissed her softly until a little of her relaxed. 'Don't you see, Katya? When you invited Tara here to give *you* a pedicure as well as me, did you think only I would kiss her? How could I be jealous if all this was a present for me?'

'You're jealous.' Katya's body tensed again. Tara placed a concerned hand on Eva's arm, but Eva reached to the side to reassure her.

'I am, but it doesn't matter. The three of us are here right now, because no two of us could satisfy each other alone. Together, we can push each other to the pleasure we're all looking for.' For emphasis, Eva edged her hands closer to Katya's basin, never dropping eye contact. 'Let me take care of your feet, Katya. Trust me with that. You can hurt Tara as much as you need to be able to endure the pleasure. Do you see?'

Katya's feet twitched, obscured by the scented water in the basin. Tara met Eva's eyes and nodded her accord. She crawled into Katya's lap with a sigh of fear and anticipation.

Eva lifted one foot from the healing bath Tara had

drawn, gazing at it with utmost reverence. She glanced up to check Katya's willingness, and saw her hands burrowed under Tara's shirt, cupping and lifting her generous bosom.

Katya's forehead wrinkled as her fingers clenched tightly around Tara's nipples and twisted. The pretty brunette's mouth opened in a silent, ecstatic cry. Eva's jealousy melted, replaced by the conviction that all was as it should be. Katya's foot rested in Eva's grasp, the weight of it a tangible sign that Eva was finally free to claim the deepest desires of her heart. Eva closed her eyes and pressed a fervent kiss to the tip of Katya's big toe. Above her, Tara screamed, and all was well.

The Fruits of the Forest
Rose de Fer

'Ach, this is really boring!'

My heart fluttered at the familiar voice. The sexy lilt, the rolled 'R's. Kirsty MacIntosh: my first-ever girl crush.

She drew up beside me and we stood there watching the groom and his ushers twirl their kilts on the dance floor in a drunken rendition of the zombie dance from *Thriller*.

The wedding reception was in full swing now. We'd served dinner and cleared away the plates and for the past half-hour we'd all been standing around outside feeling useless in our old-fashioned starched black dresses and pinafores. I suppose it was in keeping with our surroundings. Inverloch House looked just as grand now as it probably had a hundred years ago, when armies of servants had scampered around doing their Victorian masters' bidding. But the grand Lachlan-Cairncross family had presumably fallen on not-so-grand times and now they hired out their stately home for parties and weddings.

Vincent Price's laughter signified the end of the first act. Now it was the bride's turn to make a fool of herself. She looked like a giant meringue as her bridesmaids heaved her onto the dance floor and into a line with them. She took a last gulp of champagne before the music started. A familiar ballet piece that made us cringe.

Kirsty groaned loudly. 'Dear God! They're not paying me enough to stand here watching Blancmange Lake!'

I disguised my burst of laughter as a sneeze. She was right; it was a truly appalling sight.

'Come on, Emma. Let's get the fuck out of here.'

'What?' I gulped. 'You mean leave? Now?' My heart began to race with anxiety at the thought.

It was the uniform. It had a strange effect on me. It transformed my normal English reserve into something like submissiveness. The idea of skiving off while I was wearing it seemed unthinkable, like bunking off school while still in uniform, advertising to all the keen-eyed old ladies in the shops exactly which school I was profaning by my flagrant truancy.

Kirsty had no such fears. She was a free spirit, bold and brash enough to do whatever she liked and get away with it. 'They'll never miss us,' she said, confident as ever. 'I've got something I want to show you. And it's not fair of Lord and Lady Moneybags to keep it for themselves.'

'Keep what for themselves?'

'You'll have to see, won't you? Come on. The guests are all hammered anyway and no one will even know we're gone.'

I wasn't sure that our boss, Mr Carmichael, wouldn't miss us. Although I hadn't seen him for a while I could never shake the feeling that he was right behind me all the time, waiting to pounce on any little thing I did wrong. But I couldn't say no to Kirsty. Besides, there were plenty of other waitresses and most of the guests were finding their way to the bar under their own steam anyway.

'OK, but if we get caught –'

But she was already gone. I caught a flash of her radiant auburn hair as she slipped around the side of the house and headed off towards the woods. I hurried after her, suddenly not caring what might happen if we got caught. I felt like I was twelve years old again, flattered beyond reason that the coolest girl in school wanted to spend time with mousy little me. She gave me the courage I could never find on my own.

'This way,' she called, waving me over. 'The path is over here.'

'Right behind you.'

She reached the edge of the trees before I'd caught up with her. Then she pushed her way through the brambles and disappeared into the forest. After only a moment's hesitation, I followed. It took my eyes a moment to adjust to the darkness inside the shelter of the trees. Birds and squirrels chattered noisily above, telling us off for invading their domain. But Kirsty was nowhere in sight.

'Where are you?' I called.

'Over here!'

That was no help at all; I couldn't tell which direction her voice had come from. But she'd mentioned a path so I looked for one. The undergrowth wasn't dense enough to suggest there was only one passable route through the forest but I immediately spotted a muddy patch of ground with unmistakably female footprints so I followed them. Soon her voice grew clearer and I had the sense that she'd been talking to me all the while, assuming I was right behind her.

'– which is just typical of the rich snobs,' she was saying.

'Uh-huh,' I said, sure I'd have agreed with whatever it was anyway. 'So where are we going?'

'It's not far.'

Her teasing answer made me smile. There was no one else in the world I'd have gone on an excursion like this with, no one else who could tempt me to abandon my post. I was the one good little English girl on a team of fiery Scots so I was always at a disadvantage. Half the time I couldn't understand Mr Carmichael's heavy brogue and he disdained me so much he never even bothered to try and make himself clearer.

But Kirsty had taken me under her wing. She'd explained everything about the job, which was nowhere near as straightforward as I'd assumed when I applied for it. Best of all, she'd defended me fiercely to a belligerent guest on my first day of work when I gave him the wrong order. He'd had too much to drink and he called me a stupid bloody cow. Kirsty had got right in his face with such a scorching reprimand that I actually felt sorry for the poor bastard by the time she was through. He'd even apologised to me.

She'd seemed like a protective big sister in the beginning but it wasn't long before I found myself admiring other things about her. Like her dramatic cheekbones, the firm set of her jaw, the radiant brilliance of her hair. And her accent … It had seemed impenetrable on my first day of work but now I had the trick of it and it was like a beautiful foreign song. She could be crude sometimes, and she cursed like a sailor, but I still fell under the spell of her accent. I was smitten.

'Here we are!'

We emerged into a large clearing and I gazed around me in wonder. I'd had no idea what to expect but the place she had taken me to was magical. A carpet of tiny white flowers spread out across the grass in all directions and larger more showy blossoms dotted the open space at intervals. The air was heavy with the intoxicating scent of lilies and roses. Bees hummed and zigzagged among

139

the colourful petals. At the edges of the forest were fruit trees, hung heavy with ripe red apples. The trees circled the clearing like a fence and the ground beneath them was littered with windfalls.

'It's beautiful,' I said, knowing the words were inadequate to describe this little patch of Eden.

'Pure dead brilliant is what it is,' Kirsty enthused, taking me by the hand and dragging me into the clearing. 'And it's a fucking crime to keep it all to themselves.'

She released me and I closed my eyes and tilted my head back, inhaling the fresh country air, the flowers, the crisp smell of the apples. My mouth was watering. 'If I had a secret garden like this,' I said, 'I'd never spend any time in the house.'

When I opened my eyes I saw Kirsty loading her rucksack with apples. She caught me watching and gave me a lascivious wink. She didn't need to ask me – or even tell me – to keep quiet about it. I'd been brought here as an accomplice; that much was obvious. So there was no point in not joining in. I wandered over to one of the trees and plucked the plumpest, reddest apple I could find. I bit into it and sighed with pleasure as juice ran down my chin. It was quite possibly the most delicious thing I'd ever tasted.

I heard a solid crunch as Kirsty followed suit and her extravagant moan sounded positively obscene. We giggled like schoolgirls as we sat down in the lush grass and ate. Kirsty had nibbled treats in the kitchen while we were serving dinner but of course I hadn't dared. I was too afraid of getting caught. But some of Kirsty's pluck must have rubbed off on me. The only downside I could see now was in doing the time without having enjoyed the crime. I glanced down at my uniform and grinned at how we must look. Like two Victorian maids scrumping apples in their master's orchard.

I finished my apple and tossed the core into the trees. 'Sweet,' I murmured. Then I lay back in the grass and closed my eyes, savouring the riot of lovely smells and the twitter of birdsong in the trees.

And that's when she kissed me.

I hadn't even heard her approach but suddenly her lips were pressed to mine and I was struggling beneath her, shocked and bewildered and, yes, a little frightened.

But Kirsty was stronger and she pinned me down in the grass, forcing her tongue inside my mouth. I resisted only a moment more before giving in. As I relaxed into the kiss she lowered herself down on top of me, her hands in my hair, dislodging my little lace cap. She tasted like apples, rich and heady and sweet. Intoxicating.

The warm weight of her breasts against mine felt wonderful and I moaned as the kiss went on and on. I couldn't believe it was happening. I'd never even imagined such a thing with her. With any girl, for that matter. My feelings for Kirsty had been alien and unfamiliar to

141

me and something I felt I absolutely must keep hidden. I hadn't even entertained the thought of what might happen if she found out about my silly little girl-crush. It had certainly never occurred to me that she might feel the same towards me.

When she finally pulled away she closed her teeth gently on my lower lip. I had kept my eyes closed the entire time, lost in the moment. Now I was too embarrassed to open them. Afraid to look her in the eye, afraid to acknowledge that I had enjoyed the kiss, afraid to confront the possibility that she might be disappointed.

'You taste like forbidden fruit,' she said, and I could hear the cheeky grin in her voice. Her accent made everything sound irresistibly rude.

'So do you,' I managed in a hoarse whisper.

She was silent for a while and eventually I felt brave enough to open my eyes. She was smiling down at me, her head slightly cocked, reminding me of an inquisitive animal. A predatory one.

My lips were tingling. I could still taste her. And I wanted to taste her again – everywhere. I writhed gently in the grass, silently imploring her.

Kirsty took the lead again and reached out to stroke my face. A hot blush burned my cheeks as I turned my head to press my lips into her palm. I kissed her fingers and tasted apples again.

She placed her other hand on my chest and I arched my

back, wanting her to go further. I licked the tips of her fingers and then I took them into my mouth one by one and sucked off all the juice. I rolled my hips in response to my mounting excitement and the sound of my skirt rustling against the grass made me think of something waking up. Something wild that had been unleashed and now couldn't be stopped. My pussy was growing very wet at the thought of her taking me, fucking me, having me. When she finally drew her hand away she shifted her position until she was straddling me, holding me pinned between her muscular thighs.

I gazed up at her, admiring the way her hair tumbled wildly around her shoulders. She reached behind her back, unfastened the laces of her pinafore and tossed it aside carelessly. Then she began slowly unbuttoning her black dress. She made it last, taking her time and teasing me while I watched.

At last she exposed her cleavage and I squeezed my legs together at the sight of her black lace push-up bra. She had a fantastic figure, like a vintage pin-up: big breasts, tiny waist, wide hips. She slid the top of her dress down and trailed her fingers down over her breasts in a provocative display.

I wanted to touch her, to feel the creamy softness of her. She was beautiful and I told her so, my voice barely able to get the words out.

'Then touch me,' she said, taking my hands. She

pressed my palms against her breasts, guiding my movements until I was touching her the way she wanted me to.

Her sighs of pleasure gave me courage and I slipped my hands around to unfasten her bra strap. She smiled as I peeled the cups away, releasing her breasts. Her nipples were like hard little knots and I longed to kiss them. But when I tried to sit up she pushed me back down.

I stayed where she wanted me and she got to her feet. She seemed to tower over me as she slid her dress the rest of the way down. Her knickers matched the bra – black and lacy – and I wondered if she'd worn them just for me. Suddenly the little adventure didn't seem as spontaneous as I'd originally thought. Had she planned this all along?

Kirsty slid her panties down and I blushed at the sight of her full, pouting sex, nestled beneath the thinnest trail of ginger hair. Her lips glistened with moisture, with arousal like mine. She looked gorgeous standing there naked in the forest. Like some lustful wood nymph, the kind who would lie in wait to seduce unwary travellers.

She raised her eyebrows expectantly. 'Well?' she said, drawing out the word.

My face grew hot again and my courage evaporated. 'I can't,' I murmured. Suddenly I was consumed by insecurity. What underwear had I put on that morning? Had I even given it any thought or just grabbed my comfiest bra and knickers? How could I have known someone else would be seeing them?

The words 'I can't' were on my lips but I managed to swallow them down. I smiled and got slowly to my feet. She'd teased me; it was only fair that I tease her too.

I untied my pinafore and pulled it off. Then I kissed her. When she closed her eyes I looped the pinafore over her head and tied it around her eyes like a blindfold. She sighed and moved her hips sinuously in response as I caressed her naked body. I stroked her throat, drawing my fingers down over her breasts, teasingly avoiding her nipples. I was dying to touch them but I wanted to make her wait. I slid my hands down along the curve of her waist, then over the swell of her hips. Kirsty gasped as I came close to her sex but again I left her hungry.

I began to unbutton my dress as she had, slowly and teasingly. She couldn't see me but I brought her hands up to my chest so she could feel the swell of my breasts. The dress fell away and I unhooked my bra. The straps went slack and immediately her hands were pushing the flimsy material away, exposing me. She clutched my breasts in her hands, squeezing them, exploring their shape and size without being able to see them. A little moan escaped her and then she was dragging my knickers down.

I stepped out of them and kicked them away as Kirsty's hands roamed over every inch of me. Without a trace of hesitation she slid one hand up between my legs

145

and pressed her palm against my sex. It pulsed hotly in response to her touch and she laughed softly, clearly enjoying my reaction.

The air was cool against my bare skin and a little shiver ran through me as Kirsty drew her fingers along the slippery lips of my sex. When she pushed a finger inside me I cried out and my legs threatened to buckle.

Kirsty laughed again and said, 'I want to see you.' It wasn't a request. She'd let me have my teasing fun but now she wanted to be in control again. I blushed again as she removed the makeshift blindfold and took a step back, looking me up and down.

I stared meekly at the forest floor, too shy and uncertain to meet her eyes. My hands itched to cover myself but I forced them behind my back.

'Mmmm, you are a submissive little thing, aren't you?' she said. 'So wet and willing but too timid to admit it.'

My face burned again with the truth of it.

Kirsty circled me like a wild cat closing in on its trapped prey, touching and teasing me with her fingers. She slid her nails down my spine, making me arch my back with a little moan. Then she held my upthrust breasts from behind, and slid her fingers back and forth over my stiffened nipples.

'Very submissive,' she purred in my ear.

I could only sigh helplessly in response. My sex was throbbing so hard it was almost painful.

146

She didn't torment me for long. Her hands came to rest on my shoulders and she pushed me down firmly until I was on my knees in the grass. Then she returned to stand in front of me. I gazed up at her and a little shudder of desire ran through me at the sight of her towering over me. My face was at the level of her sex. She twisted a hand in my hair and I gasped as she pulled my head forwards until my nose was almost touching the thin strip of pubic hair.

She smelled like sex – musky and salty, hot and wet. I didn't hesitate. I pressed my lips against her inner thigh and slowly kissed a line up to her velvety pussy. With my fingers I spread her lips apart and licked her once with my tongue. She gasped and I felt a little shudder run through her. Her legs trembled and I kissed her again, sucking at the juicy lips of her sex, swiping my tongue back and forth across the swollen knot of her clit. I'd never been with another girl before but, since we had the same parts, I knew exactly what to do. It was both strange and exciting.

Kirsty moaned with pleasure, clutching my hair with both hands as I swirled my tongue around the soft folds, finally dipping it into her dewy slit. She was copiously wet. I pushed my thumb inside her as well, digging it in deeply to find her G spot. She gave a soft cry and tightened her grip on my hair, pushing my face hard up against her. I breathed in the rich, ripe scent of her as

I dragged my tongue up along her warm wet opening, fluttering it against her clit. In seconds she was crying out and I felt the hot spasms of her orgasm as the muscles contracted around my thumb. My own sex throbbed in response and grew even wetter.

'Oh, good girl,' Kirsty said. 'Good, good girl.'

I chewed my lip as I gazed up at her. The sun glinted off her hair and she might have been the bronze statue of a goddess, with me a faithful priestess worshipping at her feet.

Kirsty didn't say a word then. She just pushed me onto my back in the grass. I stared up at the canopy of trees, at the sunlight streaming through the branches. I felt the heat of the sun on my exposed body as she firmly drew my knees apart. Blood roared in my ears and my heart pounded with exhilaration.

She had wanted it fast and direct herself, but it was clear she wanted to draw it out with me. I was her plaything. I held my breath as I waited for her to touch me and I gasped when she finally did.

She stroked the backs of my thighs, coming teasingly close to my eager sex only to dance away again. Her touch raised gooseflesh and I shivered despite the warmth of the clearing. At last she stroked the lips of my sex and a lightning bolt of excitement shot through me. I whimpered softly, begging her to do it again, but she had other ideas. She crept up between my legs and lay on top of me. The warmth of her sex so close to mine made me flush with longing and I ground my hips against her.

With a laugh that told me she was enjoying my shameless display of arousal, she lowered her head to my breasts. She pushed them together with her hands and kissed them, brushing her lips across them, then licking them with her warm wet tongue. Every touch sent electric jolts through my body and I arched and writhed beneath her.

When she finally slid back down between my legs I was begging her to get me off. I had never been so wildly aroused in my life. If a group of ramblers had suddenly appeared in the clearing I still would have begged her not to stop.

Kirsty forced my bent knees wide apart and my legs trembled with the effort. I heard her rustling in the grass and then there was the shock of something hard and cold against my sex. I cried out and struggled against the sensation but Kirsty held me down. After a moment the chill faded as my body warmed the object. Kirsty began to press it against my sex, rolling it over my clit and making me gasp at the stimulation. At first I thought it was a vibrator but when she drew it away I blushed even more deeply. It was an apple.

She bit into it and sighed with lascivious pleasure. Then she pressed the bitten side against my sex and the rough texture was almost more than I could take. Juice trickled down over my pussy lips, tickling me. My legs tried to close but Kirsty nudged them apart again, brushed the smooth cool skin of the apple over me and then pressed the pulp up against my clit.

I tossed my head and clutched at the grass as I felt the first mounting twinges of an orgasm. Kirsty sensed how near I was. She tossed the apple aside and nestled between my legs. I gasped when I felt her tongue, lapping at the sweetness of the apple and sucking at my juicy clit. She held my legs wide apart, occasionally drawing her nails along the tender skin of my inner thighs. The sensation made my legs twitch and each time she forced them apart again.

The smell of apples was rich and ripe in the air. The memory of their taste mingled with the musky taste of Kirsty as she kissed, licked and sucked me. Her tongue fluttered impossibly fast against my clit, side to side and then up underneath, then down along the folds of my lips and back up again. I gave up trying to stifle my cries.

The climax overtook me and I screamed into the trees, my sex convulsing and pounding me with wave after wave of nearly unbearable ecstasy.

Afterwards my legs fell open and I lay splayed and spent in the grass. The trees spun dizzyingly above me and it was a long time before I realised Kirsty was talking.

I was too devastated to make out what she was saying. It might have been another language. But her wicked smile told me she was pleased with my performance. She took another bite from the apple and then she smeared its pulp over her breasts, gasping slightly at the chill against her nipples.

I stumbled to my knees and crawled to her on all fours. She held the apple out to me and I bit into it, tasting both of us. Then I lowered my head to her swollen nipples and began to lick the juice off them.

The Hungry Eye
Emelia Rawlings

I must have watched that film a hundred times now. On my laptop propped up in my single bed, one hand stuffed down my pyjamas, trying not to make too much noise within the paper-thin walls of my student flat. On my iPhone in the back row of the lecture hall, holding my bag on my knees beneath the tabletop, pressing it against me at the right moments. Just seeing the thumbnail on my computer is enough to get my clit aching for more, even now.

* * *

It was supposed to be a documentary. I'd been set an open theme for my sociology project, under the title 'Changing Attitudes'. The idea of what I would research came to me as I was browsing in the local bookshop. I'd been heading for the small collection of titles that used to be discreetly tucked away at the end of the fiction section, just after the short story and poetry books. But that had all changed since I first arrived at college. Now there was a whole bay of books on promotion, those naughty books that I liked so much, the ones that kept me warm at night in my student digs when I really should have been reading Foucault and Durkheim.

What a perfect subject, I thought, and one I'd enjoy. Has the renaissance of erotic literature changed women's attitudes to pornography in general? The dissertation would need to be presented back to the class, so I decided I would film my interviews and cut a mini-documentary from the findings. I posted a request on Facebook for volunteers and got an overwhelming response from friends, and friends of friends, and people who were just Facebook friends, nothing more.

I set a day aside for interviews on a weekend when all my flatmates were out of town. I tidied our dingy student apartment as best I could, threw some extra cushions on the sofa to make the place feel friendly and safe and pulled the voile curtains across for privacy. I set up my video camera on a tripod opposite the sofa and placed an armchair for myself just beside it so that I wouldn't be on film.

I'd made an effort to look as professional as a student on a budget can be – I wanted people to take this seriously.

It was a hot day, and I'd put on a knee-length cotton skirt and a demure blouse with buttons up to the neck. I pulled my dark hair back into a pony tail and put my glasses on, thinking as I looked in the mirror that I could cut the mustard as a professional sociologist.

The first girl was someone from my course whom I'd never really got to know. Susan was the studious type, never seen in the student bar, and I imagined that, while we were downing cocktails of a Friday night, she was probably getting ahead on her latest assignment. She'd done her homework for my interview: she quoted from the same theorists that I'd been studying for the dissertation, presented her own highly thought-through hypothesis on the subject. I wasn't after that though – I wanted to know what women really thought. As I wasn't getting anything personal from her I wound up the interview by asking if she'd read the latest steamy paperback that was hitting the bestseller lists. 'Oh, yes,' said Susan, not batting an eyelid. 'What made you buy it?' I asked, expecting her to tell me about the link between the rise of erotica and the e-book, or something similar. 'The spanking,' she replied as she rose from the sofa and shook my hand before departing.

It tickled me to think of this serious young girl curled around a good book and her right hand. As I listened to the next interviewee bang on about *The Female Eunuch*, images of Susan moaning as a chisel-jawed hero took a paddle to her plump backside kept popping back into my mind. It was a fun distraction from the polemic, not to mention an inappropriate one. But it was making me feel a little hot under the collar so I tried to concentrate on my questions and steer the subject back from the 70s to the present day.

The next few interviews were useful, but unremarkable. The heat was making me drowsy, and I was quite glad when I realised I just had one more to go.

When the doorbell rang for the last time I was surprised to find two girls on my doorstep. I'd been expecting Violet. She was on a course with my best friend, Belinda, who'd passed on my post, and I recognised her from her Facebook page. She had thick curly auburn hair that fell way past her shoulders, and she played on her Pre-Raphaelite attributes by wearing an old-fashioned floral dress that buttoned down the middle all the way to her knees. Her calves below were the colour of cream, with a light sprinkling of freckles.

She introduced her friend, Jude, to me. They couldn't have been more different. Jude was tall, with bobbed brown hair, and was wearing a skinny vest and a pair of denim shorts that showed off her lithe tanned legs. I looked at them jealously, then realised that she could see me looking, but she just beamed and put out her hand.

'Have we met before?' I said, as I shook it. She held my hand just a few seconds longer than really necessary.

Jude's voice was deep, with an accent that spoke of the best of English public schools. 'No, but we've seen you around. We were so excited when Belinda said you were looking for volunteers.' I thought I noticed a little exchange of smiles and glances between the two girls, but I didn't think anything of it.

They settled onto the sofa, looking completely at home, and started to answer my preliminary questions – where were they from, what they were studying. Violet was the chattier of the two, while Jude looked content to sit back and let her friend talk for her. As they talked, I started to notice that they would regularly touch each other on the arm, or even on the thigh, and it became clear that they were more than just friends.

It didn't bother me, but I was curious. My only gay friends were men, and I'd never really got to know any lesbians. It wasn't something I'd given a lot of thought to, but it was hard not to imagine when faced with two such beautiful women, who were obviously very into each other. I wondered what they looked like when they were making out, and the same warm feeling ran over my body as when I'd imagined serious Susan being spanked.

I tried to focus on my set of questions, and moved on to asking them why they had volunteered to speak to me.

'Oh, it's such an interesting subject, isn't it? We've always been really into porn, but we've never admitted it to anyone,' said Violet, brightly.

It wasn't the answer I was expecting. No one else had been so candid, so direct. The thought of this prim-looking Victoriana girl getting off to porn started to make my pussy tighten. I should have been asking them about ethics, but I was much more interested in what they got up to when they were watching. But I didn't want them to know what I was imagining, so I looked down at my questions with a serious look and improvised.

'What is it about porn that you enjoy?' I asked, deadpan as I could make it.

'I love the noises,' said Jude, looking me straight in the eye. 'I love hearing the slurping and smacking sounds, and the moans when a woman is really enjoying herself. Especially when you can make it happen for real straight afterwards.'

I blushed, and turned back to Violet, not knowing what to say. She wasn't planning to spare me though. 'It's the words for me,' she said, her head turned towards Jude. 'All those dirty words that porn stars use.' Then she turned to me equally unembarrassed. '"Suck my tits." "Suck my clit." That sort of thing. Just hearing them makes me so horny.'

Hearing them come out of her plump lips was making me feel horny too. I could feel my cheeks reddening, the colour spreading down to my neck; while below my pussy was swelling like mad. I wasn't sure what they were playing at, whether they were just teasing me for

157

laughs or were really trying to turn me on. The agony was too exquisite to stop, so I tried to put my qualms aside, and carried on with my made-up questions as if I was deadly serious.

'Do you watch porn together?' I asked, looking down at my notepad.

'Oh, yes,' said Jude. 'And we make it too.'

'Make it?' Oh, God! I pretended to scribble notes down in my pad, terrified of looking them in the eye.

'Yes,' said Violet. 'We love to film ourselves together. We make up stories. It feels so much more real when the camera is rolling.'

'What sort of stories?' My handwriting was a mess, my hands were shaking with excitement.

'Oh, you know,' Violet giggled coyly. 'Maybe that it's our first time, that one of us doesn't know what they are doing.'

'Or that someone's been naughty and needs a little correction,' said Jude, smiling serenely at me.

'We could show you if you like,' said Violet, as if the clever idea had just popped into her head.

My clit knotted furiously, but my mind was whirling. I opened my mouth, but no words came out.

'It would be useful for your research, wouldn't it?' said Jude. 'What a film produced by women might be like? Like the film equivalent of the mommy porn you're studying.'

She spoke in all seriousness, as if we were discussing academic methodology, and all I could do was play along. I cleared my throat and said, 'Very useful, I'm sure.' Despite my eagerness from down below, I felt horribly shy – were they mocking me? What was I supposed to do, just sit and watch? I pretended to fiddle with the camera, getting behind it and adjusting the zoom. They didn't need any more invitation.

'So, we might start just with a bit of kissing, get the place warmed up a bit,' Violet said to the camera. They turned to each other and just looked for a moment, laughing and smiling. Jude pushed the hair out of Violet's face and gently started to kiss her. They closed their eyes, and kissed for what seemed like for ever, as I watched from behind the camera. I held my breath, and could hear the moistness of their lips and the quiet 'Hmmm' that Violet sighed every now and then. Looking through the zoom, I could see Jude licking Violet's lip, and Violet opening her mouth slightly so that Jude could bite on her bottom lip. They inched a little closer, not stopping, so that their busts were touching, pushing gently against each other as they kissed. 'Mmmm, that's nice,' said Violet quietly as she pulled back for a moment, and put her hand on Jude's chest.

'It's sexy, isn't it,' said Violet, turning back to the camera, '… watching someone? What would you like us to do next?'

'I think that's up to you, isn't it?' I said, my throat clenched in embarrassment. I could only just hold myself together as it was, without being asked to join in on the act.

'I know what I want to do next,' said Jude, unbuttoning Violet's dress to the waist, and pushing the material to one side to reveal a deep-green lacy bra pushing up two creamy breasts. Through the bra, I could just make out a brown nipple, pushing hard against the lace.

Violet decided to act the innocent. She looked at Jude, wide-eyed, and gasped, 'What are you doing?'

'Don't be afraid,' Jude whispered. 'I only want to touch.' She put her hand over Violet's breast and gently rubbed the nipple through the lace.

'No, stop, please!' said Violet, acting her heart out, struggling unconvincingly.

'I think you like it really,' said Jude. 'Feel how hard I'm making you.' She pinched the nipple that was pushing through the flimsy fabric.

'I've never ... I can't ... It's wrong.' cried Violet, protesting too much.

'Just let me touch, just for a moment. Otherwise I'll tell your father what a dirty girl you've been.'

Violet whimpered. 'Please don't do that ... I'll do whatever you ask. But you'll only touch there, won't you. Nothing else. Promise?'

'I won't do anything you don't want me to,' said Jude,

pulling Violet's breast from the bra and bending her head down to kiss it. She kissed down towards Violet's nipple, and took it in her mouth to suck. Violet leaned backwards on the sofa with her eyes closed and put her hand on the back of Jude's head. Jude's lips puckered around the nipple, and I could just see her tongue flicking around it. 'Oh, that's so good, suck harder,' sighed Violet, slipping right out of character. Jude pulled the other breast out and moved her head over to the right while Violet pinched her own nipple. As Violet stretched back, pushing her breasts upward, she opened her legs and I could just see another hint of green lace between her pale thighs.

The sound of Jude sucking and Violet sighing was making my own nipples swell and harden, and I could feel concentric circles of warmth moving across my breasts, and an electric cable shooting signals down to my clit. For my own sanity, I was still trying to maintain my charade as documentary film maker. I fiddled with the zoom every now and then, and then decided to take it off the tripod and hold it in my hand.

'Good, you can come closer now if you want,' said Jude, who hadn't forgotten I was in the room. I got off the armchair and knelt down with the camera in my hand so I could get a better angle, painfully aware of the wet patch that was seeping through my thin skirt onto my calves.

Violet got up, slithered the dress that had been

161

unbuttoned to her waist down to her ankles and stepped out of it. Her breasts were still half trapped, pushed together by the green bra, her nipples hard as bullets. The knickers that I'd caught a glimpse of earlier formed a green lacy band across her hips and, as she generously twirled slowly for my benefit, across her buttocks too. Bending over for the camera, she treated me to a long look at her firm cheeks, and the little green triangle of cotton between her legs. I wanted to reach out and pluck it, to see what was underneath, but I felt rooted to the spot.

I realised that as well as twirling for me, she was performing for Jude, who was sitting on the sofa, legs apart. 'Oh, baby, you look hot,' said Jude, as she undid the button of her denim shorts and slid her hand down beneath. As Violet swayed, Jude's hand moved up and down, her mouth opening as she watched through half-closed eyes. 'Take your bra off for me, baby,' said Jude, husky as a man. Violet put her hands behind her back and unclasped the bra, letting her beautiful breasts fall free. Then she bent over and slowly started to peel off her knickers. Jude had the front view, I had the behind. As the lace moved down over Violet's buttocks, I could see the sweet pink pucker of her ass and the fullness of her lips beneath. Jude was also enjoying the show, her hand moving more frantically now. As Violet moved towards Jude, I moved around and perched on the end of the sofa to get a better view.

Violet had finished with the innocent act, and turned into teacher. She grabbed Jude's wrist and pulled it out from the open denim shorts.

'You dirty girl, what the hell do you think you are doing?' she said, slapping Jude's hand.

'I'm sorry, Miss,' said Jude, not being able to resist a smile.

'Get out of those slutty clothes immediately,' said Violet, towering over her and putting her hands on her naked hips.

Jude wriggled out of her shorts and top, and sat on the sofa in white cotton bra and panties. Her body was lithe, her stomach toned as an athlete, but her breasts were full. She looked even more tanned in the white cotton.

'Look at you,' said Violet. 'What do you call this?' She put a finger on the small damp patch on Jude's knickers, and Jude gasped with pleasure. 'Take those off right now.' As Jude began to take them off, Violet grasped a handful of her hair and pulled her off the sofa. 'Now bend over,' she ordered, as Jude's knickers fell around her ankles. She obliged, pushing her skinny little ass in the air. Violet inspected it for a moment and then slid her hand between Jude's legs.

'Oh, fuck,' cried Jude, her body jerking at Violet's touch.

'What did you say?' Violet bellowed, taking her hand away to reveal a moist set of fingers, which she promptly put in her mouth.

163

'Nothing, Miss.'

'Did you swear at me?'

'No, Miss.' Jude was pushing her ass higher in the air, itching for Violet's hand.

'You know what happens if you swear, don't you?'

'Yes, Miss, sorry, Miss,' gasped Jude.

The smack of Violet's hand against Jude's flesh almost made me drop the camera. Her hand left a white mark on Jude's tanned bottom. Violet was smiling cruelly as she administered several more blows, her cheeks reddening with excitement. Each stroke was a little harder than the last, and with each one Jude moaned and lurched and then pushed her ass back again for more.

When Violet finished, she was breathing heavily from the exertion, and she flopped down on the sofa. Jude straightened up, and then straddled her friend.

They started to kiss again, seeming to forget about me, but this time it was even sexier as their naked bodies pressed against each other. My body was going wild, and I was desperate to touch – them, me, whatever I was allowed to touch. But I held off, mesmerised by the sight of these two gorgeous women getting more and more excited.

They hadn't forgotten me though, far from it. Jude sat back on Violet's lap and looked over at me. I wondered what I must look like, with my professor glasses and my lust-soaked blushes. 'So, what next?' she said.

Squirming, I said, 'I don't know – you tell me?'

Violet smiled sweetly, cruelly, and said, 'Well, we don't know. If you don't tell us, we'll have to just stop.'

Oh, my God. I couldn't bear it. 'Suck her tits,' I said to Violet, surprising myself with the words that had sprung out of my mouth. Jude leaned forward again and let Violet take a nipple in her mouth. I came in closer with the camera, focusing on Jude's face as she closed her eyes and bit her lip with pleasure. Then I zoomed in on Violet, who was swirling her tongue around Jude's nipple, leaving a trail of moisture. I moved around and filmed from behind, watching Violet's hands clench Jude's buttocks as she continued to feast on her breasts.

I was standing now, looking down on them on the sofa. I realised they would carry on doing this indefinitely unless I gave instructions. 'Jude, lie down on the sofa with your legs open,' I said. She smiled and did exactly what I asked, showing off her pink pussy that was surrounded by little wisps of brown hair. 'Violet. Lie on top of her, and rub yourself against her. You know what I mean.' Violet obliged and lay with one leg between Jude's and one leg on top so that their pussies could meet. She started to slide against Jude, moaning as she did. 'Tell me how it feels,' I said, getting bolder now.

Jude's eyes were closed as she pushed herself against Violet's writhing body. 'Oh, fuck, that feels good, oh, Jesus.' Violet's breasts were pressed against hers, their hard nipples rubbing against each other.

'Fuck, I think I'm going to come ...' said Jude, her voice getting louder, her movements faster, more urgent.

'Wait!' I said. I couldn't bear this to be over yet, although I would be coming myself soon if I wasn't careful.

Violet slowed down and looked over her shoulder at me for my next instruction. Her blue eyes made me shiver. 'Go down on her. But do it slowly,' I said.

Violet slowly moved her body down, her hair sweeping over Jude's body, until her head was between Jude's legs. She pulled her hair back over her shoulders so that I could point the video camera at the critical spot, and she began to kiss and lick Jude's thighs. Jude was groaning now, begging her to let her come, but she wasn't doing anything until I told her to. 'Let me see her pussy,' I said, getting closer with the camera. Violet gently pulled Jude's lips aside so I could see her pink flesh and her swollen clit. I waited a moment, taking a good look, while Violet's breath over her clit was driving Jude mad.

'Suck her clit,' I said, and Jude shouted, 'Oh, Jesus, thank you!' Violet put her tongue over Jude's clit and started to lick, slowly and firmly. Jude put her hand on the back of Violet's head, as if terrified she might stop, but she kept on, alternating between little licks and sucks until Jude couldn't take any more. 'Oh, fuck, I'm coming, I'm coming!' she cried, pushing herself against Violet as she came against her willing mouth.

I let her get her breath back before ordering Violet to sit on her face. Now it was Violet's turn to scream as Jude ate her greedily. Meanwhile, I was so hot that it was time to take matters into my own hands. Filming from behind, I focused the camera with one hand on Violet's sweet ass that was pushing and thrusting as Jude licked her. As last I allowed my left hand to pull up my skirt and slide into my knickers, which were damp with all the excitement of the previous hour. As Violet jerked for the final time, shouting 'Oh, Jesus, Jude!' I let my fingers slip and slide over my swollen clit, until my whole pussy started to clench and rip in a glorious orgasm.

* * *

I didn't see them again for at least a week. I was walking with Belinda across the campus one lunchtime, when I spotted Violet's curly hair across the crowd of students heading for the canteen. She saw me and waved, her face erupting into a huge smile. I hoped she might come over, but she turned away and became lost in the crowd.

'Hey, Catherine,' said Belinda, waving her hand in front of my face to wake me from my dream. She'd seen Violet too. 'How did you get on with your documentary thingy?'

'Oh, fine. Pretty boring really,' I lied, hoping my face didn't betray me.

'That's not what Violet said,' said Belinda.

'Really?' I blushed warmly, remembering some of the other things that Violet had said.

'Yeah, she was raving about how clever you are. How good your interview technique is. She said to tell you she hopes to get to see the film when it's finished.'

I giggled to myself. A private screening was definitely in order. I couldn't wait.

School for Popular Girls
Heather Towne

Mandy didn't really want to leave her suburban high school. She had ever so many friends there – classmates and teachers.

'Yes, Mandy.' Her mother agreed with her on that point. 'But they're all *male*.' The woman looked into her daughter's pretty, open face, at the girl's slender, full-breasted body. It wasn't any wonder the sunny, blonde eighteen-year-old was so popular with the boys, and men, at her school.

Mandy blinked her big blue eyes. 'But what's wrong with that? They're all so nice to me.'

Mandy's mother sighed at her daughter's appealing apparent innocence. It was both a blessing and, possibly, a curse. 'I know, Mandy. But I worry about them being *too* nice to you. So nice that they get you into trouble. You need to have some girlfriends, for, uh, a more balanced social life.'

The woman smiled nervously at her daughter. She never had been good at these intimate talks. 'Boys are only, um, after one thing, you realise that, don't you, Mandy?'

'Good grades? A spot on the football team? Making girls laugh?'

Mandy's mother squeezed her delightful daughter's soft, slim hand. 'I've decided to send you to Wellington Academy, the all-girls school in Edson. It's only twenty miles from the city. I'll see you every weekend. It'll be a wonderful experience for you, Mandy. You'll make lots of *new* friends – girlfriends.'

Mandy wrinkled her button nose. Now, she supposed, she'd have to cancel that weekend camping trip with the boys' track team. 'Yes, mother,' she said dubiously, like the dutiful daughter she was. 'If you say so.'

* * *

That evening, Mandy's mother dropped her off at the front doors of the two-storey redbrick building that served as the dormitory at Wellington Academy. Annabelle, who was to be Mandy's roommate, was waiting inside the entrance of the building. The small, dark-haired, dark-eyed girl gave Mandy a warm hug of welcome, then took her hand and skipped up a flight of carpeted stairs with her and down a hallway to the room they would share.

'Neat, huh?' Annabelle chirped, closing the door and

gesturing with her arm at the two single beds, one closet, two bureaus, a pair of bookshelves, and a desk and chair that made up the small dorm room.

'Sweet!' Mandy enthused back. She was still rather unhappy about leaving all her old friends at the high school, but sharing a room with a girl her own age would be something special all right. And Annabelle seemed so nice and friendly.

The girl reached up and swung her arm around Mandy's shoulders. 'You'll love it here, Mandy. Everyone's so super-friendly, and the teachers are great, and you'll have all kinds of courses to choose from.'

Annabelle glanced at the thin silver watch on her tiny pale wrist. She fluttered her long dark lashes and licked her full red lips. 'Well, maybe you want to get to bed early tonight? It'll be a big day for you tomorrow. I'll join you.'

Mandy smiled at Annabelle. Maybe girls *could* be as great friends as boys, if you gave them a chance. 'That sounds like a good idea, Annabelle,' Mandy agreed.

Annabelle squeezed Mandy affectionately and then turned on the desk lamp and flicked off the room lights. Then she stood in the middle of the dorm room, unbuttoned her white blouse with the blue school crest on it and stripped the garment off. She wasn't wearing any underwear. Her small porcelain breasts glowed in the subdued light, her pink nipples sticking out a half-inch or so from the tips of her breasts.

171

Mandy swallowed, staring at the girl. Annabelle tossed her blouse onto one of the beds alongside one of the walls, and then twisted her blue plaid skirt around her tiny waist, unhooked it and let it fall down her slender legs. A triangle of neatly trimmed dark fur covered her pussy. Mandy swallowed again.

'Well, aren't you going to get undressed?' Annabelle asked, kicking her skirt over onto her bed. 'You don't sleep in your clothes, do you?'

Mandy smiled shyly. 'Oh, no, of course not.' She dropped her suitcase at the foot of the other bed along the opposite wall, then turned to face the wall and slowly and self-consciously began to pull her green T-shirt out of her skinny blue jeans. 'Um, there's no bathroom?' she said, looking at the smooth, blank, white wall.

'Not in the dorm rooms,' Annabelle answered. 'There's a communal bathroom at each end of the hallway. We all have to share. That's the spirit of Wellington Academy – helping and sharing, learning and growing. Here, let me help you with that.'

Annabelle walked, naked except for her white ankle socks, in behind Mandy, took hold of the girl's T-shirt and pulled it right up over Mandy's head. The T-shirt popped off and Annabelle sent it sailing over onto her bed with her clothes.

Surprised, but grateful, Mandy shook out her long, blonde hair, not looking around at the other girl.

Annabelle shot her fingers into Mandy's hair and stroked, smoothing the silky strands out, up on her tiptoes, her pert, mounded buttocks clenching.

'Th-thanks!' Mandy gulped.

Then she jumped, when Annabelle unhooked her white bra at the back and pulled the loops off Mandy's shoulders and the entire bra away, leaving Mandy totally nude above the waist. The girl crossed her long arms over her large breasts, blushing furiously.

Annabelle reached around and deftly popped open the button on Mandy's jeans, pulled the faded denim right down Mandy's long legs.

'Oh, thank you!' Mandy bleated. These Wellington girls *were* really helpful.

'Not a problem,' Annabelle responded, slipping her little fingers into the waistband of Mandy's white panties and tugging them down over Mandy's trim, round butt cheeks. Right down Mandy's legs.

Mandy thrashed her stockinged feet free of her puddled jeans and panties, dived onto her bed and squirmed under the covers. She tugged the white sheet and beige blanket up to her chin and flipped around so that she stared at the wall, not daring to look at Annabelle still standing there naked next to her bed. 'Well … goodnight!' Mandy gasped.

'Goodnight,' Annabelle replied. Then she slipped into the bed next to Mandy, under the covers, the two girls' nude bodies spooning together.

Mandy shuddered and gaped at the wall, feeling Annabelle's smooth, bare, heated skin against hers; Annabelle's long, hard nipples poking into her back; the girl's pussy pressing into her bum; and legs contouring to her legs. 'Um, is your bed broken or something?' Mandy asked.

Annabelle laughed, and Mandy felt the girl's small hot body convulse against hers. Annabelle slid her left arm around Mandy's left shoulder. 'No, silly. I'm just keeping you company. I know how lonely a girl can feel on her first night at Wellington – away from all of her family and friends.'

Mandy turned around and faced Annabelle in the crowded bed. 'Really?' she said, her pretty face beaming now. 'That's *so* sweet.'

'Sure. Like I said, that's the Wellington way.'

Mandy's grin widened and she flung her arms around Annabelle and hugged the naked girl even closer to her naked body. Their breasts squished together, their nipples pressing. Annabelle slid a leg over Mandy's legs under the covers so that their pussies touched as well, Mandy's blonde fur mingling with Annabelle's black.

'That's super!' Mandy exhaled, warming up tremendously to her roommate both emotionally and physically. She looked into the girl's violet eyes, feeling so happy in the girl's arms, tight together in the bed.

Annabelle kissed Mandy on the mouth. 'Isn't it?' She

kissed Mandy's lush mouth again, and this time her pink tongue squirted in-between Mandy's parted lips and bumped up against Mandy's tongue.

Mandy's face burned red, her body blazing. She *had* to show her appreciation for all of her roommate's friendliness. So, she thrust her own long red tongue out against Annabelle's, and the two girls swirled the slippery pair together.

Annabelle pulled her arm back off Mandy's shoulders and slid her pale little hands in-between their bodies and onto Mandy's breasts. She squeezed the soft, thick, smooth flesh. Mandy moaned around Annabelle's twining tongue, her breasts shimmering with heat.

Mandy just had to grab Annabelle's breasts, knead those hot, taut mounds like Annabelle was kneading her heavy masses. The girls' tongues flailed urgently together.

'Now you're getting into the school spirit,' Annabelle said, finally jerking her head back. She glided her left hand away from Mandy's heaving breast and down the girl's quivering body, in-between Mandy's legs and right onto the girl's pussy.

'Yes!' Mandy gushed, shuddering as Annabelle's fingers slid through her fur and stroked her pussy lips.

Annabelle rubbed Mandy's muff, still clutching one of the girl's breasts, tangling her tongue with Mandy's again. Mandy buzzed incandescent, perspiration bathing her forehead. She yanked her right hand off Annabelle's breast and plunged it down onto the girl's pussy, reciprocating the awesome petting.

Annabelle shivered against Mandy, her hot breath gasping into Mandy's open mouth. Mandy felt the girl's downy fur beneath her fingers, the wet, wrinkly, rubbery texture of Annabelle's pussy lips – just like hers. She rubbed Annabelle's pussy like Annabelle was rubbing hers. The girls groped each other's tits, twirling their tongues together, buffing groins with abandon.

Until Mandy suddenly squealed and spasmed, Annabelle's flying fingers tripping her swelled-up clit. Mandy shuddered repeatedly, superheated waves of bliss crashing through her body and swamping her brain. She hardly felt Annabelle jerk against her over and over, the hot squirt from Annabelle's pussy against her fluttering fingers.

Mandy slept so soundly her first night at Wellington, it was even better than being back at home. It was so much fun sharing your bed.

* * *

Mandy had a busy and exciting first day of classes. Annabelle showed her around, introduced her; ran alongside her when they were both doing laps at the end of their gym class.

'So, how do you like it so far?' the girl asked, bouncing

along in her tight white T-shirt and stretchy blue shorts, perspiration sheening her cute little face.

Mandy happily pumped her long arms and legs, her blonde hair prancing in a ponytail, her face glistening with perspiration like Annabelle's. She was wearing the same skimpy gym uniform as Annabelle, as all of the other twenty girls in the class. 'I really ... love it!' she breathed. 'Everybody's so –'

'OK, girls! That's enough!' Ms Peters, the physical education instructor, clapped her hands together.

The girls jogged to a stop, laughing and patting each other on the back and bum.

'Mandy, I want to see you in the training room! Everybody else, hit the showers!'

Annabelle good-naturedly swatted Mandy's butt, jolting the girl, making her buttocks ripple in the curve-fitting shorts. 'Uh-oh. Looks like you're in trouble now, Mandy.'

'But, but ... I didn't ...'

Annabelle and the other girls trotted off the gym floor and down the hallway that led to the locker room and showers. Leaving Mandy all alone with Ms Peters, standing in the middle of the gymnasium.

The tall, toned, tanned redhead crooked a finger at Mandy. Then she swivelled around and strode off the gym floor and down the hall that led to her office and the training room. Mandy obediently followed after the woman, her head hanging just a little.

The girl found her ultra-fit teacher standing next to one of the two massage tables in the training room. Ms Peters patted the brown-padded vinyl surface and said, 'Hop aboard, Mandy. I'm sure you're not used to so much physical activity – coming from a public school – so you could probably use a good rub-down. That way you won't be so sore for tomorrow's class.'

How considerate, Mandy thought to herself, her apprehension quickly shifting to anticipation. Phys-ed *had* been optional back at her old school. That's why she'd been huffing and puffing so badly while Annabelle and the rest of the girls had glided along.

Ms Peters stripped off her damp white T-shirt and blue shorts, pried her sneakers off with her toes. Leaving the woman totally, blazingly naked in front of Mandy. She slapped the massage table. 'Well, come on! Climb aboard!'

Mandy stared, stunned. Ms Peters' entire lithe body was a uniform golden-brown, her long arms and legs smooth and lean-muscled. She had high, firm-looking breasts with protruding tan nipples. Her pussy was as hairless and slick as the rest of her body. The woman spilled some baby oil out of a bottle and onto her hands and rubbed them together, smiling at Mandy.

The eighteen-year-old swallowed hard. She'd never seen a teacher totally naked before. Ms Peters was probably old enough to be her mother. Wellington was full of surprises.

178

Mandy tugged her T-shirt out of her shorts and slowly rolled the sweaty garment up her tummy and over her breasts and head. Then she reached back with trembling fingers, unhooked her bra and let that superfluous (for Wellington) piece of underwear fall away.

'Let's go!' Ms Peters encouraged, her breasts and pussy glistening warmly, like her mouth and eyes.

Mandy sucked in air and slid down her shorts and panties together, kicked them and her sneakers away. Then she stepped forward, and dived head-first onto the massage table. Taking the plunge, as instructed.

Ms Peters' warm, strong, slippery hands slapped down onto her back in an instant. The woman rubbed, kneaded, chopped, working Mandy's super-tense muscles, making the girl groan.

Ms Peters massaged briskly but blissfully, Mandy's body shimmering and shaking and then submerging in sensual sensation under the onslaught. Ms Peters worked Mandy's neck and shoulders, upper and lower back, and then slid her hands down over Mandy's humped, quivering buttocks, onto and up and down Mandy's trembling legs.

She really rubbed Mandy's legs, digging into the girl's bunched calves with her fingers, probing deep and stretching into Mandy's hamstrings. Mandy floated on a soothing warm cloud, her muscles and tendons relaxed and flushed like never before. Until Ms Peters suddenly smacked her butt and said, 'OK, flip over.'

Mandy's eyes stared down at the tiled floor through the face-hole in the massage table, her face suddenly burning like the rest of her glistening body. She hesitated.

Too long for the brusque, businesslike phys-ed instructor. Ms Peters levered her hands under Mandy's side and rolled the girl right over, almost sending Mandy tumbling right off the table.

Mandy safely wiggled fully back on, gripping the sides of the table. Her breasts seemed to balloon off her heaving chest, her nipples shooting skyward, exposed under Ms Peters' frank gaze. Mandy so wanted to cross her legs, because the moistness of her pussy was probably very obviously visible as well.

Ms Peters slid her hands onto Mandy's chest, gliding her firm, warm palms and long, strong fingers up the soft masses of Mandy's breasts and squeezing. Mandy looked up into the woman's shining green eyes, while her breasts surged with sensation in the woman's knowing grasp. Ms Peters bent her long neck down and sucked Mandy's jutting left nipple into her mouth, pulled on it with her glossy lips.

'Mmmm!' Mandy moaned, quivering all over, suffused with emotion, especially at her coned tits in Ms Peters' clasping hands, her nipple drawn into Ms Peters' hot, wet mouth.

The woman sucked hard on Mandy's breast, then bit into her pulsating nipple with her sharp white teeth as

180

she pulled her lips off. She bobbed her red head over and quickly inhaled Mandy's right nipple, consuming a third of the girl's tingling breast in her mouth and pneumatically tugging on that mass of electrified flesh.

Mandy gasped for air, her chest beating wildly, breasts and nipples stretching and pulsing in and out of Ms Peters' mouth. The woman shoved Mandy's tits tight together and lashed her strong red tongue across both of Mandy's throbbing nipples at once, making Mandy buck on the table.

'Gets more blood flowing,' Ms Peters explained, basting Mandy's nipples in tongue-swirls. 'Eases the soreness, if not the stiffness.' She smiled and sucked up Mandy's nipples together, almost pulling them off the girl's breasts with her lips and teeth.

Mandy blankly bobbed her dizzy head, arching her chest up into Ms Peters' mouth, her gleaming nude body bowing on the table.

Ms Peters abruptly released Mandy's glistening breasts. To Mandy, though, for a moment it felt like the woman was still gripping and sucking on her tits, the impression she'd left was so strong.

But Ms Peters' capable hands had glided down to Mandy's pussy, and her fingers were pulling the girl's flaps apart. She dropped her head lower, deep down in-between Mandy's spread legs, and sucked Mandy's puffed-up clit into her mouth.

'Omigod!' Mandy wailed, thrusting her dewy mound up into Ms Peters' face. Her clit was a pink trigger, ready to explode.

Ms Peters tugged on Mandy's swollen button with her lips. And the girl exploded.

Mandy bounced up and down on the massage table, her arms and legs vibrating, orgasm coursing up from her burst clit through her over-stoked body. She hardly felt Ms Peters' tongue licking at her slit, lapping up her welling juices; she was riding Cloud Nine too high and too hard.

'I like to get the new girls off on the right foot,' Ms. Peters double-entendred afterwards, looking down at the steaming remains of Mandy laid out on the table. 'We're a team here at Wellington. Maybe you can rub me the right way next time around.'

Though Mandy absolutely agreed with the lovely idea, she didn't even have the strength to nod her head in acknowledgment. Her muscles were as limp as boiled noodles, the girl full-body relaxed like never before.

* * *

The exciting day, her first day at Wellington, wasn't yet over for Mandy. The school principal, Dr Lange (PhD), had an interview scheduled with the girl for the end of the day.

'Just to get your impressions, and hear any concerns you might have,' Annabelle explained to Mandy in the shower room, as she helped caress the girl's body with soap. Then she gave Mandy an encouraging wet kiss on the lips and padded away, headed for her clothes and the library – a group session with some other girls.

Mandy soaked up some strength from the hot water and then towelled herself off and put on her school uniform. She walked over to the administrative building situated in the middle of the small campus.

Dr Lange's secretary, Ms Sanchez, warmly greeted Mandy. And then the tall, slim, dark-haired woman with the sultry brown eyes ushered the girl into the principal's office and closed the oak door behind the three of them.

Dr Lange got up from her brown leather chair and walked around her antique desk and shook hands with Mandy. 'So, how was your first day at Wellington?'

Mandy glanced from one friendly woman to the other. She blinked her big blue eyes, her golden hair shining under the muted lights. 'Um, it was wonderful!' she replied honestly and exuberantly. 'Just like my first night!'

'Good, good,' Dr Lange said. She ran a hand through her short brown hair, and then smoothed down her short skirt, her large hazel eyes appraising ever inch of Mandy's ripe young body in the sexy school uniform.

183

'I'm glad to hear it. You'll learn a lot while you're here. We're a liberal, open, compassionate school, but we do demand a certain level of discipline – from our students, teachers *and* administrators.' She looked at her secretary. 'Carla?'

Carla strolled over to a sideboard, opened it, took out two foot-long flexible metal rulers, walked back over to Mandy and handed the girl one. Mandy took the ruler, uncertain what was happening. She watched as Carla unbuttoned her red satin blouse and unzipped her black leather skirt.

The woman stepped out of the fallen feminine garments in just her black stockings and high heels. Mandy stared in awe. The thirty-something's body was caramel-coloured, pussy fur as black as the hair on her head, upturned breasts capped by burnt-sugar nipples. She walked past Mandy and up to her boss, Dr Lange.

Mandy's mouth dropped open, as Dr Lange shed her dark-blue suit jacket and skirt and her white blouse, ending up in just her blue stockings and black pumps. The school principal's chocolate body gleamed before the astonished schoolgirl, the fortyish woman's breasts and buttocks as lush and fleshy as Carla's were trim and taut.

Dr Lange turned around and gripped the edge of her desk. She bent forwards, her shapely legs slightly apart, and thrust out her richly mounded buttocks. 'Discipline me, Mandy!' she said. 'It's your privilege as a new student. You'll enjoy it as much as I will.'

Mandy could hardly believe her bugged-out eyes – again – or what her reddened shell ears were hearing – also again. Annabelle had told her that the administration bent over backwards for their students, but she'd never expected anything like this. The ruler shook in her hand down by her side, her body quivering, something stirring deep inside of her at the sight of her principal so rawly and raunchily exposed.

Carla took up position to the left of Dr Lange, brought her ruler back and then gently smacked Dr Lange's buttocks, showing Mandy the way. Dr Lange shuddered and gasped, her ample butt cheeks shivering.

Mandy shed her blouse and skirt like they were on fire, baring her buff body all over again. Her underwear had been left behind in a locker – she really *was* learning the ways of Wellington. The girl eagerly jumped to Dr Lange's right side, gripped the ruler in her left hand and smacked the school principal's bottom with it.

Dr Lange jerked, her bum jumping, pleased. 'Yes!' she encouraged the women, twisting her head around to glare at them both. 'Harder! Faster!'

Carla smiled at Mandy. She brought her ruler back again and then slammed it against Dr Lange's plump bottom. Mandy and the principal both jumped.

Then it was Mandy's turn. She whacked Dr Lange.

Carla whacked Dr Lange. The pair alternated their slapping strokes, Dr Lange soaking up the heated impact of the double spanking on her big, absorbent rear-end. She jerked with joy at each blow, her head tilted up and body arched, buttocks gyrating with delight.

The strikes came faster and faster, a little harder, Mandy following Carla's lead, ablaze with excitement, her eyes shining and breath coming in gasps. She gritted her perfect white teeth and smacked her principal's ass, whipping the ruler against the heavy flesh, her own breasts jumping and pussy dripping just like Dr Lange's and Carla's. The air in the office grew thick with the sharp cries of pleasure and sharp crack of metal on skin, the humid scent of sex.

Until, finally, Dr. Lange pushed up off her desk and held up her hand, swaying on her feet. The cushiony brown skin of her buttocks glowed with banked heat. 'Th-thank you, ladies!' the woman stammered, her voice quavering like her body. 'Now, to conclude our interview on an even higher note, I hope, Mandy.'

Mandy shook body and soul, her eyes wild, the red-hot ruler twitching in her hand. She quickly found herself on the blue-carpeted floor of the office, curled on her side, her head in-between Carla's legs, Dr Lange's head in-between her legs, Carla's head in-between Dr Lange's legs. A triangular daisy chain, each woman facing a wet, wanting pussy.

Mandy shivered with absolute glee when she felt Dr Lange's electric pink tongue stroke her slit. She licked Carla's steamy pussy, tonguing over the woman's thick, dark flaps, tasting her tangy juices. Carla's tight butt cheeks quivered in Mandy's pale, clutching hands, as Mandy's own buttocks trembled in Dr Lange's dark hands, as the principal lapped Mandy's overexcited pussy. And Carla mopped Dr Lange's pussy with her long tongue, her hands gripping the principal's beaten bum.

The heady smells and tastes and sensuous moaning, the expert slurping and sucking, quickly sent Mandy shrieking over the edge. She was so keyed up already by what had preceded this amazing climax to her first day at Wellington that there was no holding her back.

The girl's nails dug into Carla's buttocks, her tongue into the woman's pussy, as she was tongued to explosive ecstasy by Dr Lange. Mandy frantically lapped up the spicy juices spilling out of Carla's slit, as she squirted out her own joy into Dr Lange's face.

* * *

When Mandy reported back to her mother at the end of the week, she had to admit that the girls and women at Wellington Academy were bothering her just as much as the boys had back at her old school – but in a better way. A good, hot and bothering way.

'Wonderful!' her mother blurted. 'And there's no way you can get pregnant!'

'Huh?' Mandy inquired.

'Nothing, dear. I knew you'd like it at Wellington with all the girls. I went there myself, you know. Not long after I had you.'

Printed in Great Britain
by Amazon

42363394R00111